## THE LONDON *TIMES* ACCLAIMS
## JUNE THOMSON

"Here is a crime writer to be encouraged with shouts and cries . . .

"Two qualities chiefly provide the pleasure that Miss Thomson can give. First, she writes very well about the countryside. No blather, no romanticizing, but quiet observation plainly conducted with love, a love that comes off the page.

"Second, she understands people as well as she understands the processes of nature. Observation and compassion play their equal parts here, and especially her portrait of the Inspector . . . eschews any of those marker flags of some eccentricity which . most other practitioners rely on. He is a real person, quiet, with passions, with a listened-to-instinct, with shynesses. I am ready to join him in the unhurrying chase whenever he sets off again. But such qualities are not altogether enough for successful crime entertainment. What is needed as well, above all, is a story. And this she provides. That is the recipe for success. Bake more, Miss Thomson."

# THE LONG REVENGE

## June Thomson

BANTAM BOOKS · TORONTO · NEW YORK · LONDON

All of the characters in this book
are fictitious, and any resemblance
to actual persons, living or dead,
is purely coincidental.

*This low-priced Bantam Book
has been completely reset in a type face
designed for easy reading, and was printed
from new plates. It contains the complete
text of the original hard-cover edition.*
NOT ONE WORD HAS BEEN OMITTED.

THE LONG REVENGE
*A Bantam Book / published by arrangement with
Doubleday & Co., Inc.*

*PRINTING HISTORY*
*Doubleday edition published May 1975
Bantam edition / July 1981*

*Bantam Books are published by Bantam Books, Inc. Its trademark,
consisting of the words ''Bantam Books'' and the portrayal of a bantam,
is Registered in U.S. Patent and Trademark Office and in other countries.
Marca Registrada. Bantam Books, Inc., 666 Fifth Avenue, New York,
New York 10103.*

PRINTED IN THE UNITED STATES OF AMERICA

0 9 8 7 6 5 4 3 2 1

*for*
*Jennifer*

# 1

"Telephone!"

At the sound of his sister's voice, Detective Inspector Rudd started guiltily awake and glanced at his watch.

It was half past three on a fine Sunday afternoon in June, the first whole off-duty day he had had for a long time and he had promised Dorothy that he would cut the lawn. The lawnmower still stood where he had left it, just outside the garden shed. The warm weather, the sight of the deck-chair under the apple tree and the effect of Dorothy's heavy lunch had been too much for him. He had intended dozing off for only half an hour. Instead he had slept for nearly two hours with Cairn, his brown and black mongrel dog, asleep at his feet.

Why, Rudd thought as he heaved himself out of the low canvas seat, were roast beef, three vegetables and Yorkshire pudding, not to mention apple pie and cream, considered essential to an English Sunday, especially in summer?

"You've caught the sun," Dorothy remarked as he entered the house, Cairn at his heels.

He had, too. Glancing at himself in the mirror that hung over the telephone table in the hall, he saw that his nose and forehead were quite red. More than ever it gave him the appearance of a farmer; a healthy, frank, open look that suggested to those who did not know him very well a simple outdoor type of man with not much thought beyond the price of wheat and the state of the weather. It was a deception that Rudd himself was careful to maintain when it suited him.

"Hello?" he said, picking up the telephone receiver.

"Mr. Rudd?" inquired a voice at the other end.

It was an educated voice with a ring of authority about it; a voice, too, that Rudd thought he recognised although he could not for the moment identify it.

"Yes," he replied.

"George Hammond here," the voice announced, followed by a split-second pause that was long enough for Rudd to register who the man was.

George Hammond was one of the bigger wheels in county affairs. A solicitor with a large and busy practice, a member of several committees and Chairman of the Board of Governors of the local grammer school he was, more important still, a Hammond; one of that old and long-established family that had farmed, and were still farming, hundreds of acres of the Essex countryside. There were Hammond tombs in quite a few country churches and one particularly fine one, Rudd remembered, at Tidswell, on which the stone effigies of Sir Guy de Hammond and his lady, Isabella, lay side by side under a pierced marble canopy, he with his hands clasped on his Crusader's sword, she with her little dog at her feet.

Rudd had met George Hammond two or three times at official functions, but always in the role of Detective Inspector. Hammond's use of the plain title of "Mister" therefore surprised him.

"I was wondering, Mr. Rudd, if you'd do me a great personal favour?" Hammond was saying.

It was typical of the man that he did not wait for Rudd's reply and Rudd gave a small amused smile at his own reflection in the mirror above the telephone. Hammond was the type who would assume that favours would be performed for him. It was partly his position of authority, partly the result of breeding and upbringing and partly, Rudd had to admit, the man's own personal charm and generosity. He would put himself out to help other people whenever possible.

"It's a confidential matter," Hammond went on, "and one I can't discuss on the phone. If you're free about six o'clock this evening, I'd be very grateful if you'd come over to my place for a drink and a chat. I can tell you all the details then."

"Of course," replied Rudd.

"Splendid," said Hammond and rang off.

It was also typical of him that he should assume Rudd knew where he lived. Rudd strolled back into the garden. Dorothy had put up the other deck-chair and was sitting under the tree, reading. She glanced up as he approached.

"I suppose I ought to cut the lawn," he remarked, casting a longing glance at the empty chair beside hers. She noticed the glance and smiled.

"It's too hot this afternoon," she said. "I can do it tomorrow."

"It may still be too hot tomorrow."

"Then the lawn can wait. Come and sit down."

Rudd sank into the canvas seat with a satisfied sigh and, folding his arms behind his head, looked up at the blue sky through the leaves of the tree. Cairn, after a moment's hesitation, wondering which one of them he would choose to sit by, compromised by stretching himself out on his side between them, his soft silky flank rising and falling as he breathed, his tongue lolling out. He, too, was feeling the heat.

"I thought we'd have tea here, out in the garden," Dorothy said.

Rudd who, like Cairn, had begun to doze off, opened his eyes:

"I'll have to leave at about quarter past five," he replied. "I've got to meet someone."

"We'll have it a little earlier then," she said.

It was just like her not to question him about the telephone call and not even to ask, now that he had referred to it himself, where he was going or whom he was meeting.

He watched her through half-closed eyelids as she bent her head over her book.

There were not many women who would show such natural reticence. And it was not due to lack of interest on her part either. When he did talk to her, she was immediately absorbed, her thin and rather sad face lighting up. Not that he talked to her often. The nature of his work prevented this.

He sometimes wondered, when he had time to think about it, what her life was like and if she was happy. She looked after him and the house in the steady uncomplaining way of a woman whose chief interest is in others and Rudd realised that most of the time he took her devotion for granted.

He remembered her as a girl with long brown pigtails hanging down her back that he used to tug at; and then as a young married woman; not pretty, Dorothy had never been pretty, but she had had a pleasantly rounded figure and the soft glow of a woman totally fulfilled.

She had lost both when Ted, her farmer husband, died. It was then that Rudd had offered her a home with him. It was a poor substitute and it struck him as ironic that Dorothy, who seemed destined for a long and happy marriage and several children, had finished up as a childless widow, housekeeper to a bachelor brother.

Cairn sighed in his sleep and Rudd drifted off into a doze

Later he was awakened by Dorothy getting up and going into the house. She was seeing to a cake that was in the oven. Without opening his eyes Rudd could tell this by the warm, sweet smell that came drifting out of the open kitchen window and the rattle of the wire tray as she turned the cake out to cool.

Rudd got to his feet. Cairn opened one brown eye in the soft fur of his face; a reproachful eye that clearly said, "Must you disturb me?"

"Up!" said Rudd, nudging him gently with his foot. "Move yourself, you lazy mongrel."

The dog retreated to the path where he flopped down once again, watching with sleepy interest as Rudd pushed the lawnmower up and down.

Dorothy came to the window and made protesting signs but he pretended not to notice her. The mower chirred softly, the cut grass spurted out into the box. It smelt sharp and freshly green.

When he had finished, Rudd surveyed the lawn, smooth now and patterned with alternate stripes of light and dark, and felt a sense of satisfaction at a job done and guilt assuaged. Then he went indoors to bathe and change.

When he came down again, tea was ready in the garden. The folding table was set up on the lawn with ham sandwiches, buttered scones and the newly-baked walnut cake.

To eat enough to please Dorothy was almost as great a penance as cutting the lawn and Rudd was glad when Cairn, who knew very well that he was not supposed to be fed until much later that evening, slunk up to sit beside him, on the side furthest from Dorothy, and the Inspector was able to slip him pieces of scone and cake which the dog, perfectly understanding the conspiracy, ate very quietly, half under the table.

Then it was time to go. Rudd put on his jacket and got the car out of the garage. He regretted leaving the garden but he was curious to find out why Hammond wanted to see him. It had been almost eighteen months since he had last met the man, and that had been one of those polite, formal occasions when they talked about something non-controversial; pollution as far as he could remember, a subject close to Hammond's heart as he was Chairman of a society for the protection of rural Essex.

Rudd could understand Hammond's concern as he drove out of Chelmsford on the new bypass road, a stretch of white concrete, painful to the eyes on a sunny day, with fly-over bridges and roadside filling stations, gaudy with plastic pennons and advertisements for trading stamps and free gifts of table-mats. The countryside had retreated behind the embankments and the lay-bys, except for the glimpse now and again of fields that seemed to be growing only cabbages and sugar beet among the pylons.

At Franleigh he turned off the main road, past a new housing development of red-brick bungalows, each with a bay window and an integral garage and, at the cross-roads, took the left-hand fork on to the Helston road. Here the countryside re-asserted itself and it was strange to think that only a mile or two away hundreds of cars full of people were flashing down a major highway towards the east coast at a speed and an intensity that suggested not pleasure but a lemming-like rush towards disaster and oblivion.

Rudd slowed down to a steady thirty miles an hour, driving with the window down, enjoying the soft air that smelt of sun-warmed leaves and the view of pale corn-fields. He liked the early summer, before the freshness of spring had been quite used up and the sunlight tarnished. Dog roses were blooming in the hedges and wild scabious and ox-eye daisies were in flower on the grass verges.

Helston was far enough away from a main road not to attract many visitors, although it was a pretty place. All the surrounding farmland was still in the hands of one man, a distant cousin of Hammond's, who ran it efficiently and well. Hedges were trimmed, gates painted white, farm cottages kept in good repair. Even the cows, a prize-winning herd of Friesians, looked scrubbed and immaculate. Their black-and-white patches might have been newly coloured-in that morning.

Hammond's house faced the church, an eighteenth-century building of old brick with later Georgian additions in the way of long sash windows and an imposing porch. Rudd parked the car beside a rose bed in full bloom and, having rung the bell, was shown into the hall by an elderly maid where Hammond, a big untidy man with a cheerful face, came to greet him.

"I'm sorry to drag you out all this way," he said as they shook hands, "especially when you're off duty."

"Not at all," replied Rudd. It crossed his mind that Hammond must have taken the trouble to phone headquarters to find this out.

"Come into the drawing-room," Hammond continued. "There's someone I'd like you to meet; an old army friend of mine."

Rudd followed him across the hall to a door at the far side and, as they entered, a man who was standing at the open French windows, looking out into the garden, turned to face them.

"Rudd, this is Colonel Bravington. Felix, I'd like you to meet Mr. Rudd or, to give him his official title, Detective Inspector Rudd," Hammond said.

The two men shook hands. As they did so, Rudd made a rapid appraisal of Bravington. He was a tall, lean man, with an upright, almost stiff bearing that might have been the product of military training or of rigid self-discipline. There was a certain aloofness and restraint about him, too, and an air of determined neutrality as if he would never willingly give away anything about himself. A grey man, Rudd decided, and a man of steel. This impression was enhanced by the dark suit Bravington was wearing; the neat grey hair severely parted and smoothed down over the long skull and the grey eyes that Rudd realised, with something of a shock, as he met them, were as rapidly and accurately assessing his own appearance and personality. It was not often that the Inspector found himself subjected to this kind of scrutiny.

"What will you have to drink, Mr. Rudd?" Hammond was asking, and Rudd was almost relieved to have the opportunity of turning away from that steady grey regard.

"A whisky," he replied, "with a little water."

He would have preferred a beer but doubted if Hammond's otherwise well-stocked drinks tray would supply anything so ordinary.

"Whisky for you?" Hammond asked Bravington and then said to the Inspector, "Do sit down Mr. Rudd. I'll bring your drink over to you."

Rudd chose the sofa that faced the fireplace and sat down.

He had leisure now to survey the room. Generally speaking he did not take much notice of his physical surroundings. Given a comfortable arm-chair out of the way of draughts, a book to read and a fire to sit by in the winter, he could feel at home almost anywhere, but even he was impressed by what he saw about him.

It was a long, low ceilinged room, running the length of the house, with sash windows overlooking the front and two sets of French windows opening on to the back garden. The furniture was comfortable and shabby; deep arm-chairs and a sofa covered in faded brocade. The focal point of the room was a huge white stone fireplace with an oil painting of a landscape hanging above it that evoked in Rudd memories of his childhood. The trees then had seemed as richly loaded with leaves, the shadows beneath them as dark and dense, and the air had been full of the same brooding sunlight, ominous and at the same time exciting, that presages a summer storm. The empty hearth beneath was filled with a great mass of flowers and in front of it, lying stretched out on the rug, was a red setter that opened its eyes as Rudd sat down and then slowly got to its feet and, coming over to him, laid its chin on his knees and looked up at him with intelligent red-brown eyes.

It was a less piercing scrutiny than Bravington had given him. All the same, it had the same calm and unwavering intensity. After a moment or two, the dog seemed satisfied at what it saw and it returned to its place in front of the hearth. As far as it was concerned, Rudd was accepted.

At this moment Hammond crossed the room, handed Rudd his whisky and then sat down in one of the arm-chairs beside the fireplace. He was followed by Bravington who sat down in the opposite chair. They both half turned to face Rudd and he had the feeling that some kind of interview was about to be conducted.

After a few polite and non-committal remarks about the weather and gardens, mere conversational reconnaissance in Rudd's opinion, Hammond went on to remark:

"I believe you know Suffolk fairly well, Mr. Rudd?"

It was said in the same casual tone and yet something told the Inspector that they had got down to business at last. The interview had begun.

"Fairly well," he replied. "I usually spend my holidays at Barnston. That's a small village near the estuary of the Fletch."

"You've been going there for some time?" Hammond continued.

"Yes. For several years," Rudd said.

He was aware that Bravington, although silent, was following the conversation with interest.

"It's pleasant to go back to the same place year after year," Hammond remarked. "You must get to know the place and the people quite well."

"Yes, indeed," replied Rudd.

He stopped there, offering no more information. It was time, he felt, for Hammond to reveal the true purpose of this meeting.

Hammond looked at Bravington who gave a small, almost imperceptible nod of his head. Like the red setter, they had come to a decision. Rudd was accepted.

Hammond put down his glass on the low table beside his chair and leaned towards the Inspector.

"Mr. Rudd, what we are about to tell you is highly confidential. Whether or not you help us with the problem is for you to decide. But whatever your decision I'm sure I can trust you to keep anything you will hear from now on strictly to yourself."

"Of course," replied Rudd.

"I'll leave Colonel Bravington to fill you in with the details," Hammond went on.

Bravington turned his bleak grey eyes on Rudd.

"Hammond was quite right to stress the need for secrecy because what I have to tell you involves matters of state security. It has to do with a possible murder."

"Ah!" said Rudd and settled back comfortably in his seat.

# 2

Bravington bent down to pick up a small leather document case that was leaning against the side of his chair. Zipping it open, he took out an envelope which he handed to Rudd.

On opening it, the Inspector found that it contained three photographs, all of the same man. The first was a studio portrait, a full-face close-up. The other two were casual studies, possibly enlargements of snapshots or street-photographers' pictures. The first showed the man in a dark suit, carrying a brief-case and walking rapidly towards the camera. In the other, he was wearing light trousers and an open-neck shirt and was sitting at an outdoor café table, laughing, with a glass in his hand. The setting of the last one was, Rudd decided, probably Africa or the Middle East. The light in this photograph had a sharpness and hardness that was not English or even southern European.

Having glanced at them all quickly, Rudd re-examined them more carefully. The studio close-up showed the man's face in most detail. He was, Rudd judged, in his middle fifties. The features were strong but a little too powerful to be considered handsome. The nose was high-bridged and jutting, the eyes rather deeply set, but the mouth and chin were good. The man was smiling slightly but the smile had not touched his eyes. They looked out of the photograph with a much more ironic and mocking expression.

The other two enlargements suggested a man of above average height, broad-shouldered, still vigorous and healthy.

Rudd glanced up. Bravington was watching him closely and it was apparent he expected Rudd to say something.

"Possible victim or possible murderer?" he asked.

"Possible victim," Bravington replied.

Rudd shuffled the three photographs together and then spread them out fanwise in his hand like playing-cards. There was an elusive quality about them that he could not put into words. An unreal atmosphere? Perhaps that was what he felt about them; as if the man was playing a part.

Rudd sharpened his attention. Yes, that was exactly the impression they gave him. The two outdoor photographs reminded him of the stills you see outside a cinema, advertising the current film; while the studio portrait was of the kind an actor might send to his theatrical agent: a study of a middle-aged man who could take on the role of a ship's captain or a big-game hunter or even, Rudd thought with a faint smile, some high-ranking police officer; someone, anyway, with authority and experience, used to action and with a slightly cynical and worldly-wise attitude to life.

He handed the photographs back to Bravington.

"Not an actor, is he?" he asked.

Bravington gave him a sharp glance that was full of sudden respect.

"That's perceptive of you, Mr. Rudd. No, he isn't an actor but he's something very close to that. He's a British Secret Service agent."

It fitted, Rudd thought. An agent would doubtless have to play many roles.

Bravington replaced the envelope of photographs in his document case.

"The man's name is Alec Mercer," he said, "and we have good reason to believe that his life is in danger."

He paused and seemed uncertain for a moment how to continue; a moment of indecision that Rudd judged was unusual in him. Perhaps, not knowing the Inspector, he was unsure how best to proceed with him. But obviously he intended that Rudd was to be involved in some way. Neither he nor Hammond would have gone to the trouble of getting him to the house on a Sunday evening merely to inform him of a possible murder.

It was Hammond who broke the silence, eager to speak.

"Perhaps, Felix, you should explain to Mr. Rudd the story behind the case," he suggested.

Rudd wanted to laugh but repressed the urge. Hammond's own weakness had trapped him into making that suggestion. He was a man who enjoyed a good story himself and assumed the Inspector shared his preference. Not that Rudd objected. He was prepared to sit and listen for as long as necessary. But it was the situation as a whole that intrigued him; not just the potential murder of a man called Mercer, but also Bravington's involvement in it and the part that he himself seemed chosen to play.

"If you think that's best," Bravington replied, although he appeared only unwillingly to accept Hammond's judgement in the matter. He turned back to Rudd. "I don't want to bore you with a lot of detail about Mercer's career but you'll need to know something of it in order to understand the present position. He comes from a cosmopolitan background, English father, French mother, with a German grandmother on his mother's side. His father was a diplomat and Mercer was educated both in England and abroad. Apart from French and German, which he speaks fluently, he has a good working knowledge of several other languages, including Russian. He was recruited into the Intelligence Service in the late thirties and has been active ever since. Too active, perhaps, because last summer, on doctor's orders, he was sent home from the Middle East, an assignment he's held for several years, and posted back to London for less strenuous office duties. Not unnaturally, he found the life irksome and he made up his mind to retire early. He has private means, as I understand, and he's a very astute business man who knows how to invest his money. Anyway, he started looking for a house in the country. We now come to the nub of the matter. Not long after he started negotiations to buy it, he received this."

Once again Bravington reached into his document case and this time brought out a small, square, cream-coloured folder, in shape and size not unlike a greetings card.

Rudd examined it carefully before opening it. The paper was stiff and of good quality and the edges were lightly furred as if they had been folded and then slit along with a ruler or a knife. Stamped on the front was a small black cross. The card gave the appearance of being hand-made; the cross certainly was not professionally printed. It was slightly lop-sided and the black ink was unevenly spread. It was the kind of printing that a good amateur might make with a stencil or a lino-cut.

As he opened it, his attention was immediately caught by the photograph that was glued to the back inside page. It was not a large photograph, measuring, Rudd estimated, about four inches by three and, like the card itself, could have been produced by an amateur. It showed three men standing on what he took to be a station platform. One of the men was a railway official; French, the Inspector judged, by his uniform. The second man was a German officer, wearing the high-peaked cap and long greatcoat of the second-world-war period. The third person was Mercer, younger than in the pictures of him that Rudd had already seen, but unquestionably the same man. They seemed unaware that their photograph was being taken. The French railway official had been snapped in mid gesture, one hand gesticulating in protest, while the German officer looked on impassively. Mercer had half stepped forward as if about to speak.

What caught Rudd's attention next was the background. It was a cattle truck, its door open, and peering from the dark interior was a tightly pressed pyramid of faces, both men's and women's. There were even some children's, two or three smaller white patches appearing lower down in the black opening of the door.

On the page facing the photograph a typewritten slip of paper had been fixed.

It read:

"You will not live long to enjoy your pleasant retirement. Revenge is very sweet. When we meet again the old debt shall be repaid."

There was no signature.

Rudd looked up from his examination of the card.

"Any useful leads on it?" he asked Bravington. "Fingerprints for example?"

"I'm afraid not," Bravington replied. "I've had it thoroughly tested. The only prints on it were Mercer's own."

"What about the typewriter?"

"It's a continental make, portable; possibly pre-war but certainly old and well-used."

"And the envelope?" Rudd persisted.

"Unfortunately, by the time the card reached me, the envelope had been destroyed. You see it arrived, as I told you, about two months ago. It was delivered to Mercer's office and, when he opened it, he showed it to a colleague, a man called Carson, who happened to be with him at the time. The envelope was put in the waste-paper basket. Carson didn't get around to telling me about it for two or three days and by that time, of course, the basket had been emptied and the contents destroyed."

"So Mercer didn't bring it to you?" Rudd asked, surprised.

"No. He seemed to treat the whole thing as a joke. According to Carson, Mercer opened the envelope, started to laugh and, when Carson expressed interest, he tossed the card across the desk for him to look at. Carson himself treated it lightly at first. It was only later that he thought about it more seriously, especially in the light of an incident that occurred a few days afterwards, and it was then he decided to come to me. Mercer turned up at the office, limping badly and rather bruised about the face. It seemed the night before he'd been parking his car in the basement garage of the block of flats where he lives and was walking towards the lift, when another car reversed unexpectedly towards him and Mercer had to fling himself down against the wall to avoid being run over.''

"Did he get the number of the car?" Rudd asked.

"No, he didn't," Bravington replied. "The lighting in the garage is rather dim and it all happened so quickly. There were no witnesses either. It was quite late and there was no one else about. Anyway, Carson decided someone ought to be informed. He told me about the card and the incident in the garage and I sent for Mercer. In the course of our conversation, I discovered that, in fact, he'd received about six of these cards all together. They started arriving not long after the end of the war, in the early fifties. He couldn't remember all the details but he thought most of them had a Paris postmark, although one had been sent from Malta. And that one,'' he added, pointing to the card Rudd held in his hand, "had a London postmark. Mercer had kept none of the earlier cards which all, incidentally, had been sent to his address in Kensington. He keeps a couple of rooms there for use when he's back in England on leave.''

"Has he any idea who might have sent them?" Rudd asked.

"He says he doesn't. I questioned him closely about this but I think he quite genuinely hasn't. He seems to think it's the work of a crank, someone who has a grudge against him for his war-time activities in France and who is trying to frighten him.''

"But whoever sent the cards is now in England," Rudd pointed out, "if the last one was postmarked London. And he has, more-over, gone to a great deal of trouble to find out quite a lot about Mercer; his address in London, for example, and the fact he's going to retire shortly. That doesn't sound to me like the work of a crank.''

"Exactly," Bravington agreed. "That's why, in spite of what Mercer says, I'm treating it seriously. The other cards he received also contained threatening notes but in more general terms, along the lines of, 'One of these days I'll catch up with you.' I think Mercer got into the habit of treating them lightly and he can't, or won't, see that this one is different. It's much more specific and, as you pointed out, there's evidence from the postmark that the man is now in London. If you add to that the incident in the garage you have, in my opinion, a very real threat and one I'm not prepared to run the risk of ignoring.''

"You said Mercer thinks it might be someone who has a grudge against him because of his war-time activities in France," Rudd continued. "The photograph in the card has some connection with that, I take it?''

"Oh, yes, indeed," Bravington replied. "Mercer was so dismissive about the whole business that I didn't feel inclined to ask him too much about it though, as I was myself in Army Intelligence at the relevant time, I've managed to find out something from Records. It seems Mercer was sent into France in the autumn of 1943 on a particularly important and dangerous mission. British Intelligence had been informed that a certain hotelier in Demour, that's in the *Calvados* region, was willing to cooperate with the Allies. He was checked out and found to be reliable. From our point of view, it was an ideal set-up. The hotel, the Metropole, was a good-class place in the centre of the town which was used by Gestapo and S.S. officers so it was decided that Mercer was to be introduced on to the staff. He was given some intensive training over here in hotel management, a damned good cover story was worked out and he was smuggled into France and placed in the hotel as an assistant manager, the idea being that, as he spoke German, he would be able to pick up gossip and useful tit-bits of information from the officers who used the hotel. The town of Demour, incidentally, is and was an important centre. It's on the main line to Paris so it was used as a depot and transit point. It's also not far from the coast and on a navigable river, so it's quite a busy port as well; not for the really big stuff, but the smaller merchant ships use it. As you can imagine, a well-trained British agent had a good chance of picking up and passing on to us a lot of useful facts about the movement of German troops and supplies.

"For reasons of security, Mercer wasn't put in direct touch with the local Resistance group although he had one contact with them, some person whom he used to meet in order to pass on the information he'd collected. The contact in turn passed it on to the Maquis radio operator who contacted us. As far as possible, British Intelligence wanted Mercer to play a lone game.

"He succeeded better than they'd hoped. All the time he was in Demour he kept the Allies supplied with really vital information and he was working up a very useful contact with one particular German officer who used the hotel. It seems he put himself out to be friendly with this man and let it be known that he had strong anti-British feelings. Part of his cover story was that the family hotel in Normandy, which he should have inherited from his father, was destroyed in a British raid in which his father had been killed. He also made much of the fact that, before the war, he'd spent some time in England, working in hotels and learning the language, and that he hadn't been well treated over here. The German officer fell for this story. He, too, had been in England before the war and hadn't liked it, and he and Mercer used to swap stories about the English and their shortcomings. Mercer hinted to him that he'd liked to collaborate actively with the Germans and once or twice passed on carefully selected pieces of information that we'd fed to him through his contact. This way he won the officer's trust and the officer made use of Mercer on one or two occasions. For example, he once brought Mercer some letters to translate that had been found on a suspected French Resistance worker; that sort of thing. Mercer had great hopes of building it up into something bigger; of really being employed more openly by the Germans, which would have given him access to a great deal more information. It was a dangerous game, of course. He was likely to get it from both sides: from the Germans, if they ever discovered his true identity and, ironically, from someone in the French Resistance who, not knowing who he was, might have liquidated him as a Nazi collaborator.

"We come now to the particular incident in that photograph. The Germans had been rounding up Jews, political prisoners and Frenchmen for forced labour in Germany. The young officer that Mercer had got friendly with called at the hotel one day in the winter of '43 and asked Mercer to go with him to the railway station. It seemed there had been some confusion over a trainload of prisoners and the French railway staff were being uncooperative. The motive behind the request is obscure. Mercer himself wasn't sure why he'd been asked to go but he was of the opinion that he was being deliberately tested out and that the young officer had persuaded his superiors that Mercer might be useful to them, perhaps in their own espionage system, or possibly as a stool pigeon planted in a local Gestapo prison to eavesdrop on the detainees. There's a despatch still in existence that Mercer sent at the time, in which he analyses the possible reasons, and I think it likely that the Germans were at that time seriously considering using Mercer in active collaboration. Anyway, that's a purely academic point now. The fact is Mercer agreed to accompany the officer; they went to the station and it was there that the photograph was taken, Mercer doesn't know by whom."

Rudd examined the card again.

"It doesn't look like an official photograph," he said. "I've heard the Germans were in the habit of making pictorial records but this looks like an amateur job."

"I thought that myself," Bravington replied. "According to Mercer, there was quite a crowd of railway workers milling around as well as the German guards. Any one of them might have taken it."

"More likely to be one of the Frenchmen," Rudd said. "If it was a German soldier, he's hardly likely to want to revenge himself on Mercer now. Could it be a relative of one of those poor devils in the truck who blames Mercer for his part in the incident?"

Bravington shrugged.

"It could be; in fact, it seems the most likely explanation, but how are we possibly to find out? Thousands of people died or disappeared during those war years. Many of the official records were destroyed. As far as I can see, there's no way of identifying any of those people on that truck. I even went to the trouble of having that section of the photograph enlarged but the faces are too blurred to be recognisable."

"They presumably left for Germany?" Rudd asked.

"Oh, yes," Bravington replied. "The German officer issued a few orders, one or two of the railway staff were arrested and, I believe, later shot, and the train left."

"And Mercer stayed on, working at the hotel?"

"Not for long," Bravington said. "He was withdrawn shortly afterwards but that was purely coincidental. The local Resistance group was rounded up, Mercer lost his contact and it was thought wiser to get him out of France. It was beautifully handled. The Germans suspected nothing. You see, part of his cover story included a widowed mother living in Rouen. There really was an elderly woman, the widow of an actual hotel keeper, with a son Mercer's age. He'd escaped to England at the fall of France and we used his background. The mother wrote to Mercer saying she was ill and he was allowed permission to visit her. Later we arranged for a letter from Mercer to be sent from Rouen, explaining that she was too ill to be left and he would have to give up his job. That way we were able to protect the hotel keeper in Demour from coming under suspicion. By that time, of course, Mercer was safely over the border into Spain where he spent the rest of the war as an agent. Later, he was sent to Russia and then to different countries in the Middle East. But all that's by the way. The part of his life we're particularly concerned with is this incident in the winter of '43. I'm convinced someone has harboured a grudge against him for his part in it and is determined on revenge. Mercer won't accept this. He was very angry when I questioned him about the card. He's a very . . .'' Bravington hesitated as if searching for the best word that would most judiciously sum up Mercer's character, ''. . . *positive* person and I don't want to antagonise him. Obviously he must be protected. Our problem is how. As I see it, we can set about it two ways: either by trying to identify the man or woman (it's not impossible that it's a woman) and arrest him or her before Mercer comes to any harm; or we can try to protect Mercer from attack and hope that way to get the person who's threatening him. I'm inclined myself towards the latter course. We have so little to go on to make a positive identification. But I'd like your opinion on the matter.''

Rudd was puzzled. It seemed to him unlikely that Bravington, who must have plenty of highly-trained personnel to consult, had gone to all this trouble to seek out his opinion. There was something more to it than that but, until Bravington was ready to show his whole hand, the Inspector was quite prepared to play along with him.

''I agree that the second proposition seems the best,'' he said, ''but there's quite a few facts we can establish. The person you're looking for is most likely French and speaks and writes good English; the typewritten note tells us that. According to the postmarks, he or she has either lived in Paris, or visited there, as well as Malta and must have been in London, or had some contact over here, to find out details such as Mercer's Kensington address. Besides, the last card was posted in London. So you're looking for someone French, educated, English-speaking, who came originally from Demour and now probably lives in Paris, and has the money and the time to travel. I agree it could be a woman. A woman might very well harbour a grudge for thirty years. But I'm more inclined myself to think it's a man. After all, judging by the photographs, Mercer's still a healthy and active man. Moreover, he's used to danger. I can't see a woman tackling him, knowing this. All in all, I'd say you had quite a fair amount of information.''

''But not enough for an identification,'' Bravington replied. ''There must be dozens of French people, either tourists or on business, in London at this moment who could answer to that description, and that's assuming our suspect hasn't left already and gone to ground somewhere else.''

Rudd rubbed his chin reflectively.

"So your second course of action seems the most feasible: protect Mercer."

"And that isn't going to be easy," Bravington said. He sounded weary now, his voice almost toneless, as if the interview had taken a lot of strength out of him. "As I've already said, Mercer refuses to take the threat seriously. I've offered him protection which he refused in very strong terms. You can't protect someone against their will, especially not a man like Mercer, although I'm having a discreet watch kept on him in London. The other point is that, if we're too obvious, we might frighten off the attacker and I don't want that to happen. I learnt that lesson in the war. You must force your opponent out into the open where you can come to grips with him, and I want him to break cover soon so that we can get this whole business over and done with. My main concern is when Mercer retires. The threatening letter seems to hint that it's then that the attack will come. You remember the words? 'You won't live long to enjoy your pleasant retirement.' And it's when he retires, which he'll do in a month's time, that our real problem is going to start. I can't put one of my own men on the case. Mercer's been in the espionage game too long not to recognise someone who's been planted to keep a watch on him. Besides, I can't run the risk of the suspect noticing him as well. He may simply, then, go to ground and wait. He's waited for thirty years. Another year may not matter to him and obviously I can't keep someone tied up keeping guard on Mercer indefinitely. So what I'm looking for is someone who's already 'planted,' so to speak, who is already known in the district and accepted by the local people and who won't arouse any suspicions."

So they had come, at last, to the core of the matter. Bravington had been long enough about it, Rudd thought, but then he had been feeling his way, testing out the Inspector's reactions, asking his opinion, confirming in his own mind that Rudd was the man he was looking for. And Bravington had finally made up his mind.

"You're speaking of Barnston, of course?" Rudd asked him bluntly. It was time, he felt, to show Bravington that he was astute enough to see the situation exactly as it was. Bravington's aloof regard rested on him. For a second, he seemed a little annoyed at Rudd's directness, as if the Inspector was not playing by the rules as he understood them, and then he decided to let it pass.

"Exactly," he replied. "Mercer's bought a house in the village and is due to move in during the next four weeks. For the past few months, ever since Mercer received that card, in fact, I've been making inquiries of people I know in this part of the country. It was Hammond, an old friend from my Army Intelligence days, who came up with your name. It seems you once discussed Suffolk together and the name of Barnston was mentioned.''

Hammond smiled in a pleased way.

"I never forget a conversation," he remarked. "It's my legal training."

Now that Rudd was reminded of it, he could recall that particular conversation, too, although it was more than two years since it had occurred and had been on the most general level about summer holidays.

"Before I go any further," Bravington was saying, "I'd like to clear up one point. Is it known in the village that you're a detective?"

"No," replied Rudd. "When I'm off duty, I like to forget my official role, otherwise you're asked for the kind of advice that a policemen's supposed to be able to give; like a doctor being asked for a medical opinion at a party. They seem to be under the impression that I'm something to do with Weights and Measures."

"Good," said Bravington. He relaxed enough to give a small tight smile. "I might add, Mr. Rudd, that I've been making some discreet and thorough inquiries into your official record, and from that and what I've seen of you myself, here this evening, you may very well be the kind of person we're looking for. You're good at handling people. You've got the knack of making inquiries without being too obvious. Your approach to a case seems to be flexible. And, if I may say so, your appearance is a distinct advantage. I don't think even Mercer would doubt your innocence. In short, if you're interested, I can arrange to have you put on to this case."

It was what Rudd had been expecting but, all the same, he was taken by surprise by the offer made so bleakly and unemotionally in Bravington's clipped voice. Should he take it? Now that the moment of decision had come, he wasn't sure, and he turned to set his empty whisky glass down on the table beside him, playing for time.

The case seemed straightforward enough in the way Bravington had presented it and yet he didn't like the smell of it. There was something about it that made him feel uneasy, although what caused this disquiet he did not know.

In the silence while they waited for him to speak, a heavy atmosphere filled the room, with the same brooding intensity of the painting that hung above the fireplace. Too much, he felt, depended on his decision, and not just Mercer's life.

Hammond was looking at him, his big face with its crumpled features a little over-eager. Clearly Hammond wanted him to accept. But then Hammond had his own reasons. It was he who had recommended Rudd in the first place and, however objective he might try to be, he had enough personal vanity to wish to see his choice vindicated.

Rudd glanced from him to Bravington. His bleak eyes met Rudd's for a moment and then he looked deliberately away, turning his regard from him to the view of the long lawn and the flower beds of the garden beyond the open window.

The inference was obvious. He had no intention of influencing the Inspector's decision. In this he was being scrupulously fair and yet Rudd would have welcomed some sign from him to help him overcome his dilemma, while perversely, at the same time, he would have resented it.

It was Hammond who broke the silence.

"Well, Mr. Rudd?" he asked impatiently.

Bravington got to his feet.

"I think the Inspector would like some time to consider before coming to a decision," he said, his voice intentionally neutral.

"If that's all right with you," Rudd replied. He sounded and felt apologetic. Hammond's obvious disappointment had put him on the defensive.

"Of course," Bravington replied tonelessly. He handed Rudd a small white visiting card that was blank except for two telephone numbers.

"When you wish to get in touch with me, you can reach me at either of these numbers," he said. "The first is my office. I'm usually there between nine and six. The other is my private number. If I'm not there when you should ring, you'll be told where you can contact me. I needn't stress that I should be grateful if you did not delay too long. If you decide not to take the case, then other arrangements will have to be made. And, of course, whether you take it or not, everything that you have been told here this afternoon must be kept strictly to yourself."

"Of course," Rudd replied primly, as he put the card away in his wallet.

Bravington held out a hand for him to shake and Rudd, after a moment's hesitation, took it. It could have been nothing more than a polite gesture of farewell. Certainly the hand was cool, dry, impersonal. And yet the contact was not without some significance for Rudd. Bravington had asked for his help and offered his hand.

While accepting the one, the Inspector wondered if he was not in some way duty-bound to accept the other.

"I'll see you to the door," Hammond said a little huffily.

As he was leaving the room, Rudd glanced back. Bravington, unaware of being observed, was standing with his hands in his trouser pockets and his usually square shoulders bowed in an attitude of dejected introspection in front of the fireplace.

# 3

Over the next few days, Rudd gave Bravington's offer considerable thought. From many points of view, he could see advantages in taking it. It would be a challenge. It would be quite different from any other case he had undertaken. He would be working on his own and that, in itself, presented intriguing possibilities, for he had often found official procedure irksome. Undoubtedly too, by accepting, he might very well further his own career. Hammond was obviously keen for him to take it, and Hammond had considerable influence. So, also, no doubt, had Bravington. Quite apart from this, it would add to his own experience and the fact that the inquiry was to take place in Barnston, a village he knew and liked, was in itself persuasive.

But the disadvantages lay in these very same benefits. As it would be an unofficial inquiry, he would have no recourse to all the technical resources he had been used to: the fingerprint department, the forensic specialists, even the more humble but nonetheless useful assistance of police constables for door-to-door inquiries. The chances of failure were, therefore, greater. As a lone individual, without the weight of police procedure behind him, he could very easily make a mess of it. The responsibility of keeping Mercer alive and running his enemy to earth would be his and his alone. He jibbed, too, at involving the people he knew in the village. Although to a certain extent he had deceived them as to his true identity, it was nevertheless a place in which he could truly relax and be, to a very large extent, himself. He had friends there. To use them any further in the process of deception seemed to him to take unfair advantage of their good nature and their friendly acceptance of him.

The same ambivalence coloured his attitude to the personalities involved in the case itself. They bothered and at the same time intrigued him. Bravington with his cold reserve and bleak aloofness was a formidable yet fascinating personality and Rudd wanted to get closer to him by working on the case, if for no other motive than to understand him better. And yet, for this very reason, he tended to shy away from him. As grounds for accepting the case, it was too personal.

Mercer, too, and the man who threatened his life, held the same magnetism and repulsion. They represented a world that Rudd knew nothing about: the world of espionage, of M.I.5 and secret agents, that he had merely read about, in fiction mostly; occasionally in cases like that of Burgess and Maclean that had made the international headlines. It had always struck him as being an unreal world, childishly play-acting in some ways, with its codes and secret rendezvous; but dangerously real in many others. Rudd wondered how he could cope with men like them. He could understand the criminal mind. Even murder had its own strange logic. But he had never been able to sympathise with the type of mentality that prompted a man to take up espionage as a career and to live as Mercer had done for years, always on guard, trusting nobody, never able to reveal his true personality. It repelled him but he would like to understand it better and, if he accepted the case, he would have that opportunity. Mercer would be an interesting study for him; so, too, would be the man who sought his life.

Here Rudd felt on safer ground. To him revenge as a motive for murder was perfectly understandable; unusual, in this case, only in the length of time in which it had been prosecuted. Thirty years is a long time. The man must be very pertinacious, very single-minded. Rudd could almost picture him in his mind's eye, not as a physical presence but as a psychological force; a man prepared to wait; intelligent; cold, yet with a malicious streak in him that would, in a twisted way, get pleasure and satisfaction from the situation. A scholarly mind, too, in many ways; searching out facts; doing quiet research on Mercer over the years; preparing his thesis on him.

In short, on balance when he had weighed up all the reasons for and against, Rudd was inclined towards accepting the case. The motives for taking it were positive ones and Rudd had always preferred an active rather than a passive approach to a problem.

And yet, even at the moment of decision, he hesitated and drew back. It still did not smell right to him.

Time and time again, he came back to this irrational hesitation.

There was something basically wrong about the situation although what exactly it was he could not determine. Mercer was real enough. His story, too, must be authentic otherwise Bravington would not have been taken in by it. The photograph, too, was real. Rudd had seen it for himself, together with the accompanying threatening note. The blurred faces in the background still lingered in his mind like an after-image, human and yet featureless, with all the pathetic anonymity of the hundreds of faces he had seen in similar war-time pictures of refugees, concentration camp prisoners, displaced and suffering people the world over. Perhaps it was their anonymity that made it difficult for him to connect them with Mercer and his potential murderer. Mercer was almost larger than life, smiling out of the portrait, striding towards the camera, laughing at the café table. His enemy, too, existed in Rudd's mind as a very positive person, someone whom the Inspector could understand and, in a strange way, sympathise with.

Perhaps that was where the problem lay: in the dissociation between the blurred image and the well-defined personality.

It was his sister, Dorothy, who finally and unwittingly made up his mind for him. He was at home. Supper was over, the table was cleared and Dorothy, returning from the kitchen, found him standing at the window, looking out at the darkening garden.

He did not hear her come in. When preoccupied like this, he had a habit of cutting himself off entirely from his surroundings and she would usually withdraw into silence in sympathy with his mood, leaving him alone with his thoughts. This evening, however, she spoke to him and her voice, coming so unexpectedly, jerked him into awareness.

"You look very worried," she said. "Is there anything I can do?"

He turned towards her and, in that moment of turning, realised he was standing in exactly the same attitude in which he had last seen Bravington when he had glanced back from the doorway at Hammond's; hands in pockets, head and shoulders bowed.

Why should this realisation finally make up his mind for him? It was not sentimentality. It was not even pity. No-one could feel pity for a man like Bravington. When later he tried to make sense of it, he found that he had no more rational explanation for his decision to take the case than he had had for hesitating to do so.

It still smelt wrong. But by then it was too late. He had already telephoned Bravington.

"I've made up my mind," Rudd announced. "I'll take it."

There was no sign of jubilation in Bravington's voice. He did not even sound particularly relieved.

"In that case," he said coolly, "you'd better come up to London and we can discuss details. I'll meet you at my club. When are you off duty?"

Rudd told him he had a free afternoon two days later.

"Very well," replied Bravington and, having given Rudd the address and arranged the time of the meeting, he rang off.

The Inspector returned to the sitting-room with the thought, a little frightening but at the same time exhilarating, that, in spite of his continuing doubts, he had now burned his boats and there was no going back.

Two days later, dressed in his best suit, Rudd presented himself at Bravington's club in St. James's. It was an exclusive place, discreet and well-padded, full of dark furniture and the odour of cigars. Bravington met him in the entrance hall and took him upstairs to the smoking-room where the bright June sunshine and the passing traffic outside seemed unreal, part of another world, closed out and muffled by heavy curtains and deep-pile carpets.

They sat in a corner, at a distance from the other occupants. Bravington looked greyer than ever, Rudd thought. His profile reminded him of a bird's, with a long fastidious beak. He bent towards the Inspector, speaking in a low voice, as if in church.

"I'm glad you decided to accept, Mr. Rudd. There isn't much time to arrange matters. Mercer moves into his house in Barnston in a month's time and I want you settled in the village before he arrives. You're due for a fortnight's leave in September, I believe?"

"That's right," replied Rudd, thinking that Bravington had certainly done his homework on him.

"And you go alone? I understand you live with a widowed sister but she doesn't accompany you on holiday?"

It was more of a statement than a question. Bravington already knew the answer. All the same, Rudd seemed to be expected to verify it.

"No, I always go alone. My sister goes to stay with an old school-friend when I'm away."

He offered the remark more as an excuse for himself than for Bravington's information because he had always felt a certain guilt at not taking Dorothy away on holiday with him; not that she had ever suggested otherwise. She always seemed to be content with her fortnight's visit to Bexhill. And he needed that solitary two-weeks vacation in which to relax and be himself.

"We prefer it that way," he added, a little lamely.

But Bravington was not interested in Rudd's deeper mental processes. As long as the situation fitted his needs, he was perfectly satisfied with it.

"That's excellent," he replied. "Now we have somehow to arrange to get you to Barnston without arousing too much suspicion. I thought of sick leave but," and he paused and looked critically at Rudd's fresh countryman's face, "you look too healthy for that to work as a cover story. The simplest answer to the problem seems to me to have your leave put forward. I can get that done quite easily. A little discreet pressure put on one or two of your superior officers, without going into too much detail, and the roster can be re-arranged. Those further down need know nothing, except it's an order from those above. You're supposed to know nothing about it, by the way. You'll simply be told that your leave has been brought forward. Do you think you can look suitably surprised? How good are you at lying?"

"Not too bad, if it's in a good cause," Rudd replied with a smile. It drew no response from Bravington.

"Well, it's up to you to make it convincing," he replied shortly. "Now your leave usually lasts a fortnight. That may not be long enough for our purposes. I don't think our suspect will delay too long. He may not have unlimited time at his disposal. But a fortnight could be too short. Once that time is up, we'll have to have another cover story ready to enable you to stay on longer. There are two possibilities as I see it: a pretended accident that will keep you off duty for a few more weeks; or we could fake up some involve-ment in a local case that means you liaising with the Suffolk C.I.D. Either way I can arrange cover for you. A medical certificate would deal with one contingency; a letter from the Chief Superintendent, the other. Either excuse would satisfy your sister, I should imag-ine?"

"Oh yes," said Rudd. "She's not the type to ask awkward questions."

He shifted uncomfortably in the leather arm-chair. The business of building up a cover story was an aspect of the case he had not bargained for and it seemed to him ironic that, while he had hesi-tated to accept because the world of espionage had seemed secret and alien to him, he should now himself be involved in the same deceit that he had so smugly criticised men like Mercer for choosing as a way of life.

"Any points so far that you wish to raise?" Bravington was asking.

"There's the question of the landlord and his wife at the Plough where I put up," Rudd said. "They're used to me staying for a fortnight only. They'll need some explanation if I'm to stay longer. The cover involving the local C.I.D. won't work for them. They don't know I'm in the police. Neither will the accident. If I'm to watch Mercer, I can't pretend to be so ill that I'm not fit to go back to work."

"A good point," Bravington remarked briskly. "Any suggestions? You know them. What sort of story might they accept?"

Rudd thought quickly. Last year, Ida, the landlord's wife, had been concerned because he looked tired. He had been, too. It had been a heavy year.

"They might swallow a vague story about general ill health," he said. "Nothing too specific. Just overwork and doctor's orders to get as much fresh air as I can. I could back it up with some detail about extra leave that I'm owed."

"Do you think it'll work?" Bravington asked.

"They'll accept it," Rudd replied, feeling uncomfortable. Of course they would accept it. George and Ida had known him for years. They'd have no reason for suspecting him of lying to them.

"Any problem about changing your booking?" Bravington asked.

"No, that'll be all right," Rudd replied. "I haven't arranged for a room yet. The Plough never gets full, even at the height of the summer. I shouldn't have any difficulty this early in the season."

"Fine," Bravington replied shortly. He seemed bored with the trivia of the case and was eager to get them dealt with as efficiently and quickly as possible.

"Now I'd like to discuss the case with you in broader detail," he went on. "You know the village. You've got the reputation of bringing a bit of imagination to bear on the facts which is exactly what I'm looking for. I don't want some heavy-footed policeman marching about asking obvious questions. I was impressed also, when I first met you at Hammond's, by the manner in which you seemed to be feeling your way into the mind of the man who's threatening Mercer's life. Given your knowledge of the place and something of the man's psychology, how do you think he'll set about it?"

There was some new quality in Bravington's manner that Rudd had not seen before. At Hammond's house he had been the aloof stranger, concerned only with telling the facts of Mercer's case and,

at the moment of decision, withdrawing deliberately so that the
Inspector should feel quite free to make up his own mind; while at
the beginning of the present interview he had been brisker, much
more the efficient security official, making plans, arranging cover
stories.

Now he was genial and disarming, treating Rudd on a man-to-man
basis. On purpose, of course. Rudd wasn't fooled by the confiding
attitude that Bravington had now assumed. Nor was he flattered by
it. Bravington was a manipulator. He used people, men like Mercer
and Rudd.

It suddenly occurred to the Inspector that Bravington's concern
for Mercer's safety was not for the man himself. Bravington was
worried for other, less personal reasons. It was not Rudd's place to
understand the motivation nor did he sufficiently sympathise with
Bravington's type of mind to comprehend fully what lay behind his
actions. But he guessed that compassion, gratitude, humanity played
a very little part in it. If he had to put a name to it, it would be some
wide vague generalisation that had to do with ideas rather than
people. Security, perhaps. The State. The System.

Rudd realised that Mercer could not be allowed to die because
that would be awkward. Questions would be asked. It would be an
embarrassment for people like Bravington whose anonymity had to
be preserved. They could not allow, as Bravington had said, heavy-
footed policemen marching about asking awkward questions.

It was important that Mercer should be protected and that the
man who threatened him be quietly rounded up because the threat he
presented was not so much to Mercer but to men like Bravington and
all they stood for.

Rudd relaxed. With that now clear in his mind, he felt much
more at ease. He liked to know the terms on which he was working.
He liked to know, too, when he was being used. Not that it made
any basic difference to his attitude to the case and the people
involved in it. It did not even change his estimation of Bravington.
Rudd thought none the worse of him. He was what he was. But it
gave the Inspector a certain inner satisfaction to realise that he now
had the measure of the man.

"How do I think he'll do it?" he asked, repeating Bravington's
question. "I know how I'd do it. The village is small. Any stranger
is certain to be noticed. I'd lie low but get to know the lay-out of the
place as unobtrusively as possible and I think I'd wait until Mercer
moved in so that I'd find out something about his routine and
movements. And then . . ."

"And then what?" Bravington asked.

Rudd hesitated. It was true that to some extent he understood the mind of Mercer's killer. He had thought about it deeply over the past few days but there was much that remained obscure.

"He's waited for thirty years," Rudd said slowly, at last. "He'll have his plans perfected before he finally strikes. And I can't see him doing it at a distance. I think he'll want the satisfaction of confronting Mercer before he kills him."

"What makes you think that?" Bravington asked. He tilted his head slightly to one side as he spoke, inviting the Inspector to continue but reserving his own judgement.

"Because he has gone to the trouble of finding out a great deal about Mercer, as if he wanted to know the man thoroughly. It could be simply that he's very efficient but I've got the feeling that there's something more to it than that."

He looked at Bravington and suddenly grinned.

"Are you a fisherman?" he asked.

"No," said Bravington sharply. He seemed put out by the question.

"Neither am I," Rudd replied. He was enjoying the situation now. "But I used to know a man for whom fishing wasn't just a hobby, it was more a way of life. There was an old pike that used to lie up in a certain pool near his village. Many local men, quite good fishermen, too, had tried to catch it but it always escaped them. It was cunning, you see, and it knew the ways of men better than they knew the ways of the fish. But this man I was telling you about was determined that one day he'd get it and in the end he did. Shall I tell you how? He made a study of it. He watched it for a long time, got to know the places where it hid up, the times it came out to feed. He watched the movement of the water, too: the shallows and the eddies; and got to know the places on the bank where a man could stand and not cast a shadow. You might say that, in a way, he came to think like that fish, and in the end he was rewarded with the sight of it wriggling on the end of his line.

"I think the man we're looking for is like that. He won't give up until he has Mercer hooked. And, like that fisherman I was telling you about, it's not the death itself that matters. He could have poisoned that pike if he'd simply wanted it dead. No, the important thing was the stalking of it and the death was the final triumph to that, the culmination. That's why I think our man will want to meet Mercer face to face. And in his place I'd use a gun. It's more certain than a knife. But one thing I'm sure of, he'll look Mercer in the eyes as he pulls the trigger."

He stopped abruptly and Bravington raised his eyebrows at him in query.

"Something wrong, Mr. Rudd?" he asked.

"Yes, there is," the Inspector replied. "Something badly wrong. I've suddenly realised that it doesn't add up."

"I don't understand your objection," Bravington said a little stiffly. "As a theory, I thought it made perfectly good sense."

"But the facts have to fit the theory," Rudd pointed out, "not the other way round. And there's one fact that doesn't fit in: the incident in the garage. That certainly doesn't square with the idea of the killer wanting to confront Mercer. You don't reverse a car, hoping to kill a man."

"But he might have done so on an impulse," Bravington said. His face had closed down again. As far as he was concerned it was a mere detail and Rudd was being a nuisance in bringing it up for discussion.

"Not as I understand the man," Rudd replied. He was being stubborn and he didn't much care. He was arguing with a superior and he didn't much mind about that either. The smell of the case had come back to him even more strongly and he had the feeling that there was a great deal more to it than he had so far uncovered or even imagined existed beneath the surface.

"This man knows Mercer. He's warned him his life's in danger. He must have realised Mercer would be on his guard . . ."

"But as I've already told you, Mercer doesn't take it seriously," Bravington said with formidable patience.

"The killer doesn't know that," Rudd replied sharply. "What he must know is that Mercer's a trained agent; an agile man, quick on his feet . . ."

"I appreciate your concern," Bravington interrupted him, "but I think you're stepping outside your brief, Mr. Rudd. As far as I'm concerned, the case is quite straightforward. Mercer has to be protected. While he remains in London, that is my responsibility. As soon as he moves to Barnston, it is yours. The significance of the incident in the garage is not within your jurisdiction. I have been presented with certain facts: a letter threatening Mercer's life and what appears to be an attempt on it. It may have been an accident. It may have nothing at all to do with the case. But that is not my concern any more than it is yours. It is my job to make decisions on the facts as I see them."

"Assumptions," said Rudd.

Bravington looked at him coldly.

"Very well, then; assumptions. But may I point out that you, too, have made assumptions? You assume the killer will attack Mercer face to face with a gun. I agree, as a theory, it seems to make sense. But if we take the same facts and look at them another way, isn't it possible he may stage an accident in which he will appear to take no blame?"

"Run Mercer down in a car, you mean?" Rudd asked.

Bravingon permitted himself a weary smile.

"In a sense, he's been running him to earth for thirty years. He might try to do that quite literally."

Rudd lifted his shoulders in a gesture to indicate at least temporary acquiescence.

"I may be wrong," he admitted.

And so might you, too, he added to himself.

"You may, of course, withdraw from the case," Bravington added. "It's not too late to change your mind."

This time he did not turn away but kept his cold grey eyes fixed on Rudd's.

"No," said the Inspector. "I don't wish to do that."

Because that would mean admitting defeat and the relationship between the two men was no longer neutral enough for Rudd to admit to anything of the sort.

There was a small pause before Bravington answered in which Rudd caught a glitter in Bravington's eyes that he could not analyse. Triumph, perhaps? A quiet insolent satisfaction at getting his own way? Perhaps even a touch of admiration at Rudd's tenacity. Rudd was not sure and the next second, anyway, the glint had gone and the grey eyes were as cold as ever.

"Good," Bravington said, getting to his feet. "I'm glad you've decided to help us. You have my telephone numbers should you need to contact me, although I'm sure you won't need telling that you should do so only when absolutely necessary and then discreetly, where you can't be overheard."

"Of course," Rudd replied.

Again the cool dry hand was offered for him to shake. The gesture was purely formal on both their parts and, as Rudd left the room, he did not this time attempt to look back.

Closing the heavy mahogany door behind him, he descended the stairs, with their dark red carpet and polished brass rail.

It was a relief to emerge into the street where the typists in their bright summer dresses were going home at the end of a day's work. Normal people leading normal lives.

Well, he thought, as he hailed a taxi, he was committed now and only time would tell which of them was right.

# 4

Bravington must have put the wheels into motion immediately after Rudd's meeting with him in the club because, two days later, the Inspector was summoned to Detective Superintendent Davies's office.

Davies looked up with an apologetic air as Rudd entered.

"I'm sorry to have to spring this on you with so little warning," he said, "but it seems the Chief has taken it into his head to alter the annual leave roster. God knows why; some private scheme of his own that he's not coming clean about. The point is, he says it'll be 'convenient' to him if you'd bring your leave forward; then he won't have to shuffle the other dates around too much. Can you manage that?"

Several times Rudd had rehearsed his reaction to this very request, anticipating the moment, and had tried the different expressions and variations of reply that he could most convincingly make. Now that the time had come, he was surprised to find he spoke quite naturally.

"It's a bit short notice," he remarked. He even managed to sound slightly aggrieved.

"I agree," said Davies. "I'm willing to take it up further with him but . . ."

"Orders being what they are," said Rudd, finishing the sentence for him and giving him a grin to show he had no ill feeling against Davies personally.

"Exactly," Davies replied. "I know you're a fairly easy-going type. That's probably why the Chief's picked on your leave to tinker about with. He knows you won't start shouting the place down, demanding your rights, or offering your resignation in a huff. Not like some I could mention.''

"When does he want the dates changed to?" Rudd asked, remembering that this was supposed to be a complete surprise to him.

"The last week of June and the first week of July. It gives you about three weeks to alter any arrangements you may have made. Is that sufficient?''

Rudd shrugged.

"It doesn't make a lot of difference to me. I usually stay at a country pub and, as I haven't booked a room yet, there won't be any complications there.''

"And do you think you'll be able to get in on just three weeks' notice?" Davies asked.

"Possibly," Rudd replied. "If not, there's plenty of other pubs or small hotels. I'm not fussy as long as the beer's good. All I want is a couple of weeks' peace and quiet and if the bed's comfortable and there's decent food, I don't much mind where I stay.''

He thought it best to make no mention of Barnston. If he had to stay in the village longer than a fortnight, it might be more convincing if Davies was under the impression that Rudd had taken a room there with no prior knowledge that it was Barnston or even Suffolk that he intended visiting.

"If it's really not putting you out," Davies began. He seemed relieved that the Inspector had accepted the changed dates without too much fuss. Glancing across at the window and the sunlit view of the opposite buildings, he added, "Actually, if this fine weather continues, it may be to your advantage.''

"That's true," agreed Rudd and, as he left the office, he thought how smoothly it had all been arranged.

In front of his colleagues, he made a little more of it than he had done for Davies and grumbled convincingly enough about those in authority throwing their official weight about to satisfy their sense of honour on such occasions. For his sister, he had to make no such pretence, presenting it to her as simply a matter of orders that had to be accepted and she took him at his word, although, to ease his own conscience a little in the matter, he made her telephone her friend that evening to tell her of the change of dates and to arrange that her own visit could be brought forward to coincide with his altered plans. Later when she was busy in the kitchen and could not overhear, he telephoned the Plough to book his room for a month, giving as explanation for this extended visit the excuse he had already thought up, some extra days holiday due to him and his doctor's advice to have a longer holiday than usual.

He heard nothing more from Bravington and he did not attempt to get in touch with him. Presumably Bravington knew that the arrangements had gone according to plan. He was not the person to leave that kind of detail to chance. Meanwhile Rudd tried to put out of his mind any thought of the case. Further speculation about it seemed pointless. He had taken it on and, although his disquiet about it did not die down, he learned to thrust it to the back of his mind. It would be time enough to worry about it when he arrived in Barnston and the real business of the investigation began.

On the Friday evening before his leave was due to start, he came home to find that Dorothy had already laid his clothes out for packing; the old, comfortable jackets and casual shirts that he always took on holiday. As he stuffed them into a suitcase and looked out a few books to read in bed he realised that, for the first time since Bravington had suggested his involvement in the Mercer case, he was looking forward to it with something like pleasurable anticipation.

The next morning he set off, taking the main road to Colchester and then on to Ipswich, where he turned off into the network of secondary roads that wound through the pleasant Suffolk countryside. The hedges grew tall again and through gateways he caught glimpses of fields of corn and barley.

In the little market town of Fletchford, he eased the car over the narrow stone bridge that spanned the river and turned left on to the Barnston road. About five miles further on, the tower of the church became visible among the trees and the first houses began. He slowed down and drove gently into the village. There was no need now to hurry. He had the enjoyable sensation of a man coming home.

To anyone just passing through, it gave the impression of a small, compact village; a cluster of houses and cottages of various periods, grouped round a triangular piece of grass in the centre of which stood the war memorial. There was the Plough, the post-office, the general grocer's, the village hall and the garage that had once been a smithy and still remained relatively unchanged in appearance except for the addition of a single petrol pump outside. Only the initiated knew the little lanes and side-roads that ran behind the green that led to other houses tucked away behind high hedges.

The Plough stood at the far end of the village, sideways on to the road, with its own gravel forecourt. It had once been a farmhouse and still retained some of its original features in the three steep gables and small casement windows. Tradition said that the farmer's wife, who brewed an excellent beer, had made an additional living by selling it to the locals and that the wooden benches and tables that stood outside dated from that time.

It contained two bars: the saloon, comfortably furnished with low arm-chairs, and the public bar that had an uneven brick floor and old high-backed wooden settles that generations of backsides had polished to a fine gloss. An "L" shaped counter served both bars, behind which the landlord and his wife, George and Ida Plummer, presided with friendly hospitality.

George must have heard Rudd's car as he drove round to the back of the pub to park it in the big, open-ended barn that served as a garage because, as the Inspector got out, carrying his suitcase, the landlord was at the door to meet him.

"Well," he said, in his slow Suffolk speech, looking Rudd up and down in a humorous way, "I can't say you look all that badly."

Rudd had said little to him over the phone when he booked the room, except he needed extra vacation this year. With Mercer to keep a watch on and his would-be killer to run to earth, he could hardly plead chronic ill health as an excuse for an extended holiday.

"There's nothing much wrong with me that fresh air and a bit of exercise won't cure," Rudd replied lightly. "And Ida's cooking," he added.

George winked at him and patted his own well-developed stomach.

"There's twenty-five years of her steak and kidney pudding gone into the making of that," he said.

Rudd laughed. He liked George Plummer. He was a big, easy-going man in his fifties who, despite his size, was surprisingly quick and light on his feet. Although he never seemed to hurry himself, the pub was run smoothly and efficiently even at its busiest times. He could pull a pint of beer, hand over change, wipe down the bar counter and still go on talking to a customer without once seeming to lose his unruffled, smiling calm.

It was his wife, Ida, a small, dark, darting woman, who dashed about, emptying ash-trays, collecting up dirty glasses, washing up furiously in the small sink behind the bar.

George treated her with amused affection.

"Look at her," he'd say, "rushing about like a dried pea in a colander. Keeps her slim though and a good thing, too. There'd not be room for two of us my size in bed."

"I'll take you up to your room," George was saying to Rudd. "You'll have a cold snack in the bar afterwards, will you, same as usual?"

It was a long-established custom that Rudd ate in the saloon at lunchtime and had what Ida called a "proper hot meal" in the evening, eaten alone and rather formally in the tiny dining-room in the Plummers' private quarters at the end of the house. He would have preferred the kitchen, comfortable and homely, with its big Aga cooker and scrubbed wooden table, but he understood Ida's wish to keep that part of the house to herself. It was here she cooked and baked and conducted one-sided arguments with Dotty, the woman who came in daily to help with the cleaning and the washing up.

"Dotty by name and dotty by nature," Ida sometimes said of her in her less friendly moments.

As Dotty, a small smiling elderly woman, with as much vigour as someone half her age, was stone-deaf, such remarks passed unnoticed. Besides, she had her compensations, the singing of hymns in a high cracked voice as she worked and the frequent cups of tea she made for herself and which she drank sitting by the stove, her skirts turned back, warming her old knees. From her point of view, the work at the Plough was easy. She had, after all, brought up six children and nursed her farm-labourer husband through his last illness, and the kitchen of the public house was warm and cosy compared to her own damp cottage. So she was perfectly content.

Rudd had been given his old room, at the end of the house, with its casement window overlooking the far side of the village to a distant view of water-meadows and the far-off flash of sunlight on the river. As he unpacked, he kept glancing out of the window, pleased to rediscover the clumps of trees in their old familiar settings and the black-and-white cows, at that distance as small and as static as a child's toys, still feeding in the lush green pastures.

The top drawer of the tallboy stuck as it had stuck other years and, as he wrenched it open, the Inspector smiled. He liked it. He liked it all, from the wash-basin in the corner with its old-fashioned brass taps to the high bed with its faded red cover.

He moved about the room, taking his time, laying claim to it slowly. His pyjamas were tossed on to the bed, his dressing-gown hung behind the door and the books he had brought with him were piled up on the bedside table beside the lamp with its cracked vellum shade.

When everything had been put away to his satisfaction, he went downstairs to the bar where he ordered a pork pie and salad and a pint of bitter from George.

"Anything new happened since I was here last?" he asked, as George handed him his beer.

George leaned his massive hairy fore-arms on the bar and pondered the question.

"Old Mrs. Massey's passed over, her that had one of the old people's bungalows," he said. "And there's been a couple of weddings; nobody that you'd likely know, though. And the Threadgolds have sold up and gone to live near their married daughter in Ipswich, so there'll be someone new moving in."

Rudd drank some beer and tried not to look too interested.

"Didn't they have that white-painted house in Tiler's Lane?" he asked.

Ida, who had joined her husband at the bar and was drying glasses as if her life depended on it, broke in,

"That's right. Well, it's sold."

"Really?" said Rudd. He cut off a piece of pie and ate it slowly. "Anyone local?"

George gave a laugh.

"Londoner," he replied. "A man named Mercer."

"Seems nice enough," his wife added.

"Early yet to say," George said prudently.

"He's only been in here the once," Ida put in. "Retired, he told me. Civil Service. Wants a bit of peace and quiet."

"They're all the same," George said. "Can't wait to get out of the towns and into the country. Not that I blame them. I wouldn't give you tuppence for a house in London."

"There's been talk, too, that Mr. Thurleigh's been thinking of moving out," Ida continued.

Rudd put down his knife and fork and looked at her with genuine concern. He knew John Thurleigh well. Over the years that Rudd had been coming to the village, he had built up a real friendship with the shy and retiring schoolmaster. A widower, whose wife had died three years before, Thurleigh taught in a private boys' school at Hassett, a few miles away, and Rudd enjoyed visiting him in his house, full of books and pieces of old furniture collected over the years. If he moved, Rudd would miss the man's company. The village would not be the same without him.

"Well, that's not certain," George was saying. "He put the house up for sale last autumn and then changed his mind, seemingly.

He told Rose, at the post-office, that he was finding the garden a bit too much for him."

"He would, with that leg of his," Ida added sympathetically.

Thurleigh had a stiff leg that caused him to walk with a pronounced limp. He never referred to it and Rudd had not liked to ask him how it had happened. Gossip in the village said it was caused by an attack of polio when he was a child. It still gave him pain, especially if the weather was at all damp or cold and, on occasions, Rudd had seen him wince and rub it gently.

"Besides," Ida went on, "he must find that house hard to run, since his wife passed on."

"Now there was a nice woman," George added.

Rudd nodded. He remembered her with affection; a gentle grey-haired woman. The Thurleighs had been a devoted couple.

"I must call in and see him," Rudd remarked.

Two more customers entered the bar at that moment and Rudd took his plate and beer mug to a table to be out of the way.

As he ate, he thought about Thurleigh. He had intended calling on him anyway but the news that he might be leaving the village made him decide to see him that evening. Before doing that, he had already made up his mind to have a close look at the house that Mercer had bought, Threadgold's place, before the man moved in.

He strolled along there after lunch. Tiler's Lane was a narrow road that ran behind the church and contained a few detached houses, spaced out and standing in large gardens. Mercer's house was the last. Beyond it the lane continued with only fields on either side, except for the opening to a hard-surfaced track that led to a farm.

It was an early Victorian house of white-painted stucco, set well back from the road behind high hedges.

Rudd glanced in through the open gateway as he passed and was disappointed to see a builder's van parked outside in the drive and signs of workmen about the place. Through the open front door came the sound of hammering and there was a pile of sand by the steps.

He walked on without stopping. It would not be possible to look the place over but there was a chance that, by approaching the house from the rear, he would still get a good idea of its layout without being seen.

Here too, though, he was frustrated. Having climbed a gate into a field and walked back in the direction of the house, Rudd found that it was effectively screened from view by a narrow overgrown spinney and, after crashing a little way into the bushes, he decided he was making too much noise and retreated. However, the brief glimpse he had of the house was enough to tell him that it was some distance from its neighbour and well protected on all sides by trees and bushes.

Thoughtfully he made his way back to the village where he called in at the post-office, ostensibly to buy a book of stamps but with the intention of pumping the postmistress for information.

Luckily the shop was empty and Miss Craddock, a busy, talkative woman, was pleased to see him again and have the excuse for a chat. By degrees, he worked the subject round to summer visitors.

"I was asking," Rudd continued, elaborating on the idea as Miss Craddock was well known for taking a lively interest in other people's business, "because I've heard a friend of mine might be down here for a few days."

"What's your friend look like?" she asked inquisitively.

"Fairly tall, about my age," Rudd replied, improvising quickly.

"Why doesn't he stay with you at the Plough?" she asked.

It was a reasonable enough question but, all the same, he cursed her silently for making his falsehood more complicated than it need have been.

"I think he'd prefer to camp," he said, "or perhaps stay at a cottage or a farm."

She shook her head.

"I've not heard nor seen any stranger about the place, except for the gentleman who's bought Threadgold's house, Mr. Mercer. He was here a few days ago, seeing the builders," she said.

"They've been busy in the house for some time, have they?" Rudd asked.

"Oh, yes, ever since it's been bought by Mr. Mercer. He's having a lot done to it, seemingly."

Rudd turned the conversation to other matters and, as soon as he decently could, left the shop, with Miss Craddock's promise that if she heard any news of Rudd's "friend," she would let him know.

One thing was evident, Mercer's presence in the village had not gone unnoticed, even though he had not yet moved into the house, and although no other stranger had been seen this did not rule out the possibility that the man who threatened Mercer's life had not already looked the place over. On balance, however, Rudd was inclined to discount this. For one thing, the builders had been busy in the house and, as Rudd had found to his cost, it was impossible to make a proper investigation with them there. He did not think that the man would slip up on a detail like that. After all, he had gone to considerable trouble to find out a great deal about Mercer and Rudd thought it more likely that he would wait until Mercer had moved in before finding out the lie of the land. It was the theory that he and Bravington had agreed was the most likely.

On the other hand, he could not entirely count on this. It was possible that the man might arrive sooner, looking for somewhere where he could remain hidden until the attack on Mercer took place and, with this in mind, the Inspector intended in the next few days making a thorough search of the village and the surrounding countryside for any signs of the man's presence or, failing that, for the likely places where he might hide up when he did arrive. He dared not risk waiting until Mercer's arrival. There was no guarantee that the man might not attack straightaway and then make his escape.

He returned to the Plough in a depressed mood. Already he was finding the case difficult. It was like playing chess in the dark. You waited and waited and were not even sure that your opponent had made a move.

Later that evening, after dinner, he strolled back into the village to call on John Thurleigh, a little cheered by the thought of seeing him again.

Thurleigh's house faced the green. A light was on in the hall and the door was opened to Rudd's knock by the schoolmaster who was delighted to see him.

"Come in, come in!" he said, his haggard face lighting up. "This is a pleasure. I had no idea you were in the village. Your usual summer holiday?"

Rudd made light of his own supposed illness, although he felt he ought to mention it if only to give credence to his extended visit. Thurleigh himself looked so strained and worn out that the Inspector had guilty qualms about his own excellent health.

"You're looking tired yourself, John," he remarked, as they went into the sitting-room.

"I am a bit," Thurleigh admitted. "It's getting near to the end of the school year and everyone's feeling a little jaded."

He had aged a lot since Rudd had last seen him. His fine hair had gone thin on top and there were deep lines across his forehead and between his eyebrows. His limp, too, was more pronounced. Rudd had noticed this when Thurleigh came to the door.

"I'll make some coffee," Thurleigh was saying.

"Let me help you," Rudd said and, despite the schoolmaster's protests, followed him into the kitchen.

"I'm afraid it's all rather a mess," Thurleigh said apologetically. It was clear this was the reason why he had not wanted Rudd to accompany him. Dirty saucepans stood in the sink, unironed shirts were piled up on a chair and a bundle of old newspapers, destined for the dustbin, still stood by the back door.

"I'm afraid I get less and less able to cope with it all," Thurleigh went on, running one hand through his thinning hair and looking harassed.

Now that he saw him in the bright overhead light in the kitchen, Rudd noticed that Thurleigh's appearance also showed signs of neglect. He had always looked slightly untidy, being more interested in books, but, when Mrs. Thurleigh had been alive to care for him she had seen that his clothes were brushed and his shirts properly ironed. Now he had a distinctly crumpled and unkempt look.

Rudd felt a surge of pity for the man that he knew Thurleigh himself would not welcome. For, in spite of his diffidence, his loneliness and his apparent lack of worldly success, he was a proud and very private person who did not seek compassion.

It had been on the tip of the Inspector's tongue to ask him about the sale of the house and then he changed his mind. If Thurleigh had thought about moving out it was probably, as he himself admitted, because he found it more and more difficult to cope with it. And Rudd believed he understood Thurleigh's reasons for changing his mind without having to ask him.

He had once told Rudd that he had come to the village as a newly-married man, shortly after the end of the war. Thirty years is a long time. He had put down roots in this place; he would not find it easy to change.

The time element suddenly struck Rudd as significant. It was about thirty years ago that Mercer must have first come into contact with the man who was now seeking to kill him. You can build up a lot of hate, or love, in that length of time.

# 5

During the next four days, Rudd systematically searched the village and its surroundings for any sign of the arrival of Mercer's killer or for likely places where the man might hide. He went about it carefully, anxious not to arouse suspicions, ostensibly taking casual walks that took him to neighbouring farms and the outlying woods and fields. One thing seemed to him certain. The man would want to keep under cover but would not want to hide up too far from the village. He would keep, Rudd reckoned, within walking distance of Mercer's house. A car is a large object to hide and an unfamiliar one seen in the neighbourhood would raise comment.

It occurred to him that the man might camp but although he searched every possible site, there was no indication anywhere that someone had been sleeping out. He chatted, too, to farmers and farm labourers, leading the conversation round gradually to summer visitors, as he had done with the postmistress, but no-one had seen any strangers nor had anyone asked for rooms in any of the farm-houses or cottages.

On the Wednesday morning Rudd moved his area of inquiries to the north side of the village, the part that he could see from his bedroom window of the Plough. It contained a couple of farms and a few houses, occupying a mile-wide strip of cultivated land before the flat water-meadows began and then the saltings.

It was an easy area to search, presenting an uninterrupted vista of green, broken only by an occasional willow tree and the drainage ditches that sliced across the land. On the far side the horizon was hidden behind the long, high bank of the dyke, for the river Fletch was tidal and, particularly in winter, rose high and would have flooded the surrounding fields.

Rudd picked his way carefully across the saltings for, despite the hot weather, the ground underfoot was still spongy in places. Tussocks of coarse grass formed drier patches and he strode from clump to clump. The wild flowers were different here, he noticed; shore-side plants: sea lavender and sea asters, thrift and salt wort, while tall reeds grew in the wetter hollows.

When he reached the base of the dyke, he rested there for a few moments, getting his breath back. From this point, the view of the village was the reverse of that he had from his room in the Plough. In fact, he could see the steep, tiled roof of the public house and the flash of sunlight on glass that he took to be his own window. At that distance, the village looked compact and secure, surrounded by trees, a rural fortress in the bleaker and more open aspect of the marsh.

When he had rested, Rudd began to scramble up the steep side of the sea-wall. The grass here was sun-dried and slippery, not easy to climb, but at last he reached the top and the narrow path that ran along it.

For a moment he stood there looking about him. The dyke stretched away in both directions. To the right it led downriver towards the estuary and Rudd knew there was nowhere along it that a man could hide until he came to the village of Blair, five miles down stream. It did not seem likely that his quarry would choose a hide-out so far away.

On his left, the sea-wall curved to follow the course of the river and it was in that direction that Rudd began to walk. Further along, hidden from sight by the bend in the dyke, were some huts that Rudd remembered noticing in other years when he had walked here.

The tide was out and the river was reduced to a mere muddy stream in the middle of a shining waste of mud although, nearer the bank, where the low summer tides had not reached it, it had dried out into a complex mosaic of cracks, scattered with pieces of parched seaweed and the small brittle sun-bleached corpses of crabs. Here and there, rotten posts jutted out, all that was left of the jetties of long ago when the river was still navigable as far up as Fletchford and many of the local men kept small fishing boats. The river had silted up slowly over the years, the jetties had rotted away and the men had turned their interest away from the estuary and back to the land.

The huts came into view as he rounded the curve of the dyke.

They too were relics of the old fishing days when they were used to store gear. The first two were so dilapidated that Rudd walked past without stopping to examine them. The third, a little distance from the others, was in better condition and he scrambled half-way down the bank to where it stood on a shelf that had been cut out of the side of the sea-wall. It was a small building, not much bigger than a large box, made of tarred wood and roofed with corrugated iron. There was a tiny window that had been boarded over. The door faced the river and a flight of rough steps led down to the edge where a few stumps remained of the original landing-stage.

He noticed the padlock as soon as he approached it. It was new and still shiny. The salt air had not yet had time to rust it.

Rudd stopped in his tracks and glanced upwards. The top of the sea-wall was deserted. Beyond it, on the landward side, the hut would be invisible except for the peak of its roof. There was no-one either on the opposite bank of the river. He was completely unregarded except for some sea-gulls that were perched on the stumps.

Walking up to the door as if he was treading on egg-shells, Rudd laid his ear against the wood and listened for several minutes but no sound, not even the faintest creaking of a floor-board or a rustle of movement, came from inside. The hut appeared to be empty.

He examined the padlock next. The screws that fastened it to the door-frame seemed the easiest to tackle; the wood was rotten and whoever had put the lock there had found difficulty in screwing it home. Taking a penknife from his pocket, Rudd gently removed the screws and, using his handkerchief so as not to blot any fingerprints that might be on the metal, he pulled the fastening to one side. The door could now be opened.

The interior was dark except for the faint light that filtered in through the cracks and knot-holes in the wood. Opening the door wider, so that more light fell inside, Rudd peered round the door without attempting to enter.

He could see now that it had been recently occupied. Someone had rough-swept the floor and piled up some rubbish, old tins and wooden crates, in the far corner. On the floor, against the opposite wall, an air-bed with a blanket folded on top of it had been placed and beside it stood a candle stuck into the neck of a wine bottle.

There were footprints in the dust on the floor-boards but too faint, Rudd reckoned, to be identifiable. He wondered if there were fingerprints on the bottle. Possibly so. Whoever had occupied the hut must have thought his hiding-place inviolable.

If this had been a normal case, Rudd would have known exactly
what to do. He would have called in the experts to examine the hu
and its contents. He would have started door-to-door inquiries in the
village. But, in this investigation, his hands were tied. He wa:
merely a minor Civil Servant, on holiday, with no real officia
powers, and he dared not run the risk of stepping outside hi:
accepted role.

Pushing the door closed and replacing the screws that held the
padlock in position, he scrambled back up the slope of the dyke to
the path. The hut would have to be watched, of course, but, as he
looked about him at the level fields and the mud-flats, he wondered
how that could be achieved. Even the cows were conspicuous. A
man suddenly appearing in that open landscape would certainly be
noticed straightaway. He walked on, thinking over the problem.

Half a mile further, a grassy embankment led down from the
dyke to a raised causeway that crossed the marsh and the water-
meadows and continued as a clinkered lane past a farm, to emerge
eventually in Tiler's Lane, two hundred yards from Mercer's house.
Rudd glanced at his watch. It had taken him just over a quarter of an
hour to get from the hut to the lane. Mercer's enemy had chosen his
hide-out well.

It was in a mood of great uneasiness that Rudd started off up
the lane towards the village. And there was another feeling just as
strong; one of bafflement. It suddenly occurred to him that he was
up against someone very clever; someone who did the unexpected,
who hid in the open because that was the safest place to hide.

His uneasiness was increased when, on passing Mercer's house
and glancing in at the gateway, he saw a dark-green Rover parked
outside the front porch behind the builder's van. Intuition and a
sense of foreboding told him it was Mercer's car. The man had
probably come down from London to supervise the alterations to the
house.

Rudd halted for a moment in the gateway and then walked on.
There was no action he could take. Bravington had made it quite clear
that Mercer must not be told of Rudd's part in the investigation. All
he could do was walk on, trusting that the presence of the workmen
would give Mercer some protection and that the man who had
occupied the hut was no longer in the district. He would return
though. Of this Rudd was quite certain.

When he got back to the Plough Rudd got his car out of the
barn and drove out to Fletchford, where he telephoned Bravington at
the office number he had been given.

There was a few moments' delay and then Bravington came on the line. Rudd briefly described the discovery of the hut. Bravington was silent for what seemed a long time and then at last he asked, "Any chance of having it watched?"

"Not unless you've got someone who can do a fair imitation of a cow. Or a sea-gull," Rudd replied. "The place is as flat as the palm of my hand."

"I see," said Bravington bleakly.

Rudd could hear him breathing at the other end of the line.

"And I think Mercer's in the village now," Rudd continued. "At least, there's a Rover parked outside the house."

"It's Mercer's car," Bravington replied. "I've had a discreet watch kept on him this end and I'd heard he was coming down to Barnston."

"For how long?" Rudd asked. His voice was a little sharper than he intended but he felt that Bravington should somehow have informed him of this fact.

"Only for the day," Bravington said. "He's got an appointment later this evening in London. Look here Rudd, you don't think he's in danger right at this very minute?"

"I don't know," admitted the Inspector.

"But I gather he only decided to come down to Barnston this morning. There was some problem with the builders. The man we're looking for can't have known that."

That was true. All the same it did little to relieve Rudd's anxiety.

Bravington continued. "I know this is a very difficult assignment and, if you pull it off, I'll see that it doesn't go unnoticed."

He paused but, as Rudd did not reply, he went on. "Is it possible that we could keep a watch on this hut from the river? Or, failing that, do you think you could keep it under surveillance yourself? I'd rather not introduce anyone else into the area unless I really have to. If you don't think either of those suggestions are feasible you'd better phone me back and we'll have to re-think it."

"Very good," replied Rudd and rang off.

He was not impressed by Bravington's veiled promise of promotion. If anything, it only added to his disquiet. Rudd had a very shrewd idea of people's characters and, if he had read Bravington's correctly, he was not a man who would normally hold out that sort of inducement. He must, therefore, be extremely worried to have done so in this case.

It was in a very thoughtful frame of mind that he drove back to the village. The Plough was open and he went into the bar for lunch. For a time he chatted with George at the counter and then, as more customers arrived, he took his plate of ham salad and his pint of bitter to a corner table and began to eat, after exchanging greetings with the newcomers.

They were two farmers whom Rudd knew only by sight and they remained standing at the bar, one of them telling an interminable story about the sale of some cows. George made his usual soothing remarks and the other farmer, who seemed to have heard the tale before, merely drank and nodded his head when appealed to by his companion.

Rudd, busy with his own thoughts, hardly listened. In his imagination, he was retracing his morning's walk, trying to remember every feature of the landscape that might offer cover to a man. There were the other huts. One had almost collapsed, but the other, although without its roof and much of its back wall, might be used. And then he dismissed them. They were too near the third hut. Anyone hiding there could be easily spotted.

He needed to think of somewhere between the hut and the village, along the causeway ideally, where a man could keep watch unseen and yet have the dyke in clear view. The unknown assailant would be certain to use that path into the village. Rudd could not imagine him picking his way across the marsh, especially in the dark, with its boggy patches and drainage ditches.

At this point, the door of the bar opened and Rudd, glancing up, broke off his thoughts. The man who had just entered was Alec Mercer. There was no doubt about it. Rudd recognised him at once from the photographs that Bravington had shown him.

The Inspector's first reaction was one of absurd relief that he was still alive; absurd, because from what Bravington had told him the man who sought his life could not possibly have known that Mercer was going to be in the village that day. His second reaction was one of curiosity; it was the first time that he had seen Mercer in the flesh.

He was not as tall as Rudd had imagined him to be; more compact; but nevertheless, the athletic build was evident in the broad shoulders and purposeful walk. His face, too, was older. The studio photograph had suggested a well preserved man but, seeing him at close quarters, Rudd was aware of the tired muscles in his face and the dried-out and slightly leathery skin of someone who has spent some years in a hot climate.

All the same, he was undoubtedly a personality to be reckoned with. He carried with him an aura of strength, of being a person of consequence and, as he approached the bar, the farmer fell silent, turning to look at him curiously, and George heaved himself off the counter and stood upright, ready to serve him.

Rudd felt it safe to examine him more closely. Mercer's back, in an old green tweed jacket with leather patches on the elbows, was presented to him. His hair, he noticed, was thick and turning grey.

Intuition made him glance down at his plate again almost immediately. Although Mercer had appeared not to register Rudd's presence as he entered the bar, some sixth sense warned the Inspector that he was now aware of being watched. He half turned his head in Rudd's direction and his shoulders stiffened. Rudd promptly got on with his lunch.

Mercer was ordering a pint of bitter and two cheese rolls. His voice was deep, educated, friendly and yet curiously unreal, like a man who was acting a role. Rudd chewed and thought about it.

The impression he had had on first seeing Mercer's photographs returned to him more strongly. Mercer was playing a part in which the old tweed jacket, the hearty tone of voice, the pint of bitter and the cheese rolls were all involved. It was the role of the English countryman, thoroughly at home among fields and farms, familiar with village pubs and local landlords.

It had not fooled Rudd and it did not fool the two farmers standing at the bar. An uneasy silence fell over them. Only George seemed genuinely friendly as he pushed the pint of beer and the plate of rolls across the counter.

"How's the house getting along?" he asked.

"It should be finished by the week-end," Mercer replied. "At least I hope so. I've arranged for the furniture to be moved in on Saturday."

"Cudlip's is a good firm," George remarked. Cudlip had been the name on the builder's van that Rudd had seen parked outside Mercer's house. "Small but reliable. They'll not let you down."

He added for the benefit of Rudd and the two farmers. "This gentleman's taken over Threadgold's old place."

"Oh ah," said one of the farmers, not giving anything away and Mercer, as if aware of their reticence, took his glass and plate and sat down at a table across the room from Rudd.

There was no avoiding his eyes now. Rudd met them deliberately and nodded to him, as one does in country pubs, and, having finished his own lunch, lit a cigarette and leaned back against the wall to blow smoke at the ceiling. He was amused to notice that the farmers had formed a huddle at the bar, in which George had joined, bending his head forward to meet theirs. The story of the cows was resumed but in a more subdued manner. Mercer, for all his tweed jacket and friendly voice, was not to be included in the conversation. Ida appeared briefly. Somehow she must have got to know of Mercer's presence. Her head bobbed up behind George's while she had a look and then she disappeared again.

Rudd got up slowly and walked towards the bar, carrying his empty plate and glass. It was time, he felt, to establish his position in the place for Mercer's benefit as someone accepted and at home there. The farmers edged aside and let him in.

"Nice piece of ham, George," he remarked. "I enjoyed it."

"I'm glad of that, Mr. Rudd," George replied. "Ida bakes it with cloves and a bit of bay leaf. It's an old recipe she got from her mother."

"I'll have another pint," Rudd went on. He turned to the farmers. "You'll join me?" he asked them.

They accepted his offer. George pulled pints for all of them including himself, at Rudd's invitation, and the four men took their first gulp in silence.

Then George mentioned the cows and the farmer took up the story again. Rudd listened and made the right responses, seemingly absorbed, but he could not resist, from time to time, glancing in Mercer's direction as if casually.

Rudd's acceptance in the group had not gone unnoticed by him. It would take Mercer time, as it had done Rudd, to become at home in the place. It is not easy to establish yourself in a country community and Mercer was still very much the outsider. Rudd wondered if he realised this. He had, after all, spent many years abroad in that necessarily lonely and dangerous position of an agent. He would surely find an English village quiet and unexciting.

But it was not this that concerned Rudd at the moment. If he was to get to know Mercer, then he must have some tangible benefit to offer the man and what could be better than an introduction into the community? Mercer had almost finished his lunch and the Inspector thought it time to make it even more clear that he belonged here. Yawning and putting a hand to his face, he said to George,

"The sun's made me sleepy. I think I'll go upstairs and have an hour's nap this afternoon."

"I don't blame you," George replied. "I'll be doing the same myself as soon as it's time to close."

Rudd sauntered to the door that led to the private part of the pub, resisting the temptation to take a last backward glance at Mercer. Knowing George, Rudd was certain that as soon as he left the room the landlord would make some comment about him, if it was only, "Nice gentleman Mr. Rudd is. Been coming here for years."

At the top of the stairs there was a landing with a window that overlooked the road and Rudd stationed himself by it, keeping well back out of sight behind the curtains. He did not have long to wait. A few minutes later Mercer appeared in view, walking briskly with that purposeful air that had been apparent in the street photograph. Rudd watched him go. The man's strong back presented a broad and conspicuous target and it suddenly occurred to the Inspector that, if his instinct was wrong and Mercer's killer should not feel the need to meet him face to face, then nothing would be easier than to pick him off at a distance with a powerful high-velocity rifle and to make a get-away before a search could be organised.

It was in a very thoughtful frame of mind that Rudd turned away from the window.

# 6

Rudd waited for two days before returning to the hut by the river and then, on the Friday afternoon, the day before Mercer was due to move into his house, the Inspector set off again across the fields, as he had done on the first occasion.

But this time he was more cautious. Instead of walking along the top of the dyke, he scrambled down the far side of it, so that he was invisible from the fields, and made his way along the river bank. He had taken the precaution of borrowing a pair of field-glasses from George in the hope that, if anyone saw him, he would be taken for a harmless bird-watcher. The glasses would also be useful for surveying the hut from a distance before he approached it.

The tide was low, as it had been on the previous occasion, a mere narrow channel of sluggish brown water running between the wet mud-flats. Rudd kept as close as he could to the edge of the dyke, where it met the river bank and where the sun-dried mud formed a hard surface to walk on. But here and there little channels of water cut into it and he was forced up the slope, to clamber crab-wise along it, clinging to thick tufts of grass, the binoculars banging awkwardly against his chest, while the cows in the water-meadows on the opposite bank raised their heads and watched his clumsy progress with bovine interest.

The river curved, the sea-wall curving with it. The huts were just visible further on. Rudd sat down and, putting the binoculars to his eyes as if watching for wild-life, swept the further bank before turning the glasses in the direction of the huts.

There was no sign of life in any of them and, after a few minutes, he got casually to his feet and walked towards them. As he passed the first two, with their broken doors, he could see they were empty. He could also see that as hiding-places they were quite unsuitable. They were so near to the third hut that anyone concealed inside them would not remain unnoticed.

He walked on towards the third hut. It appeared unchanged from his previous visit but, all the same, he was taking no chances. Sitting down on the grass beside it, he lit a cigarette and leaned back in the shadow it cast across the sea-wall, as if glad of its shelter from the sun and, as he smoked, he listened for any sounds within.

He had particularly good hearing and, more than that, a keen sense of the presence of another person. But there was no sound from inside the hut, no creak of floor-boards and no weight of atmosphere of a hidden presence, only the gentle gurgling of the water in its channel and the soft sucking sound of the mud as it imperceptibly slid and shifted under its own pressure. A lark sang, too, piercingly loud above him, invisible in the almost white dazzle of the sun.

Rudd stubbed out his cigarette and approached the door. He had come prepared this time with a screwdriver from the toolbox of the car and, in a matter of seconds, the padlock was removed and he could open the door and look inside.

The hut was exactly the same as it had been before. The bed had not been used, the candle was the same length and there were no traces of recent footprints in the dust.

Replacing the screws, he felt in his pocket and brought out a length of fine fuse wire which he had bought that morning in Fletchford and, kneeling down in the grass, he looped the wire over the bottom hinge, stretching it as taut as he could. A clump of dock leaves growing near the base of the hut hid it from sight but, even without them, Rudd doubted if it would be seen.

He straightened up and smiled with satisfaction. It was a simple yet effective trap. Anyone opening the door would bend or snap the wire. There would be no need from now on for him to remove the padlock to find out if the hut had been used.

Although he was relieved to know the stranger had not returned, he was puzzled all the same and, as he walked on towards the causeway, he wondered why the man had gone to all the trouble of providing the hut with means of lighting and a bed and yet had not occupied it for the past two nights. Perhaps he had found somewhere else to hide up. Or perhaps he had moved away from the village for the time being, intending to return at a later date once

Mercer was established in his house. If this was so, the wire would warn Rudd of his return.

There was a third possibility: that the man had seen Rudd when he made his first visit to the hut and had been frightened away. As he considered this, Rudd did not know whether to be pleased or sorry. On the one hand, Mercer's life might no longer be in danger; on the other, there would be no chance of ever catching his would-be attacker. Of course, he might be only temporarily frightened off. He had waited thirty years for his revenge, after all. He could very well be prepared to wait one more year, until he felt he was quite safe, as Bravington had pointed out.

On balance, though, Rudd was inclined to think he did not know the hut had been discovered. The Inspector had been very careful to leave behind no traces of his examination and it did not seem likely that he had been seen. As he found to his own disadvantage, the countryside offered no cover, for the man himself or for anyone that Bravington might send to keep a watch on him.

He reached the causeway and examined the surroundings again, using the binoculars to sweep the level fields that stretched unbroken to the boundary wall of the distant farm. The only possible cover was that provided by the tall reeds that grew in the deeper irrigation ditches but, as they were full of water, they could not be used as hiding-places unless a man was prepared to stand submerged up to his waist. The farm, too, was out of the question. Even if the farmer agreed to have someone concealed in one of his out buildings, it might lead to talk in the village and, anyway, the farm was too far from the hut for an adequate surveillance to be kept on it. As for Bravington's suggestion of a boat on the river, that had been impractical from the start. Anyone standing on top of the sea-wall had an uninterrupted view up and down stream and, besides, at low tide, as Rudd had seen, the river was reduced to so narrow a channel that a boat would become virtually useless, isolated between the flats of deep mud that stretched for many yards on either side.

There seemed no answer to the problem except for Rudd to keep a watch himself on the hut as best as he could, strolling out to it as if casually every few days to make sure that the wire remained untouched. It was a far-from-perfect solution but the only one that he could think of under the circumstances.

He was approaching the farm and, as he passed the gate, he glanced into the yard. Although the man must have passed by it on the way to the hut with his bedding roll, Rudd could see why it was unlikely that he had been noticed. The farmhouse was set a long way back from the lane and sideways to it so that one gable end, with a window on the ground floor, faced in that direction. And between the house and the lane was a range of out buildings effectively blocking the view. A dog was sitting in the yard, quietly scratching itself, but it did not bark as Rudd went past. Yes, it would be easy for someone to slip past the farm under cover of darkness, especially if he kept to the grass verge, thus deadening his footsteps.

At the end of the farm drive, Rudd turned left into the lane that led past Mercer's house. The builder's van had gone, the drive was empty and, on an impulse, Rudd decided to take the opportunity of looking round the place before Mercer moved in the following day.

On the far side of the garden, the lawn gave way to a tangle of bushes and after a quick glance up and down the road to make sure he was not seen, he pushed his way through a narrow gap in the laurels that bounded the garden, emerging into an overgrown shrubbery. The house was just visible through the branches, a worn foot-path leading towards it.

Rudd approached warily. There seemed to be no-one about. The house had a closed-up, secretive look about it, the windows staring blankly outwards. A shaggy lawn stretched between the shrubbery and the drive and Rudd crossed it quickly, making for the back of the house where he would be out of sight of the lane.

It was an enclosed garden, surrounded by the thickly-grown spinney that Rudd had tried to push a way through on his previous visit. Perhaps it was the crowded trees that gave the garden its sinister air. That and the silence. There seemed to be no noise at all. The heat, too, was trapped in it, heavy with the scent of the catmint and verbena that had overgrown the herbaceous borders and that, without a breath of wind to stir the air, added to the feeling of oppression.

At that moment something scuttled away under the bushes and Rudd, startled, spun round. It was only a bird but the unexpected noise had been enough to make him jump. He suddenly felt very exposed, standing there in the middle of the lawn with the brooding trees and shrubs all around him, and it occurred to him that Mercer could not have chosen a worse place to retire to. The house was isolated and some distance from its neighbours, the garden ideal for a marksman to hide in. He could pick Mercer off as he strolled across the lawn or sat outside on the paved terrace behind the house. Perhaps Mercer really did not take the threat against his life seriously. Or perhaps he thought he could deal with the danger himself.

Rudd felt a stir of anger against him that was quite unreasonable. After all, it was his job to protect him, even though Mercer made it very difficult for the Inspector to accomplish this.

The facade of the house faced him. Rudd walked along the terrace, peering into the windows in turn. There was a long room first, with windows at the far end overlooking the front; then a smaller, squarer room with French windows opening on to the terrace. Next to it was what he took to be the dining-room, as a serving hatch communicated with the kitchen next door which was already equipped with an electric cooker and a refrigerator. Otherwise the rooms were empty of furniture although they seemed to have been newly decorated, for a faint smell of fresh paint was discernible above the scents of flowers and leaves from the garden. The windows in the upper storey were presumably bedrooms, with a bathroom with a frosted glass window over the kitchen.

He turned thoughtfully away. It was a large house for a single man to occupy and he wondered if Mercer was proposing to have domestic help. If it was to be a living-in servant, then Rudd's task would be considerably lightened. Even a daily woman working in the place would mean Mercer was far less vulnerable to attack.

Ida supplied the information he was seeking. He found her in the kitchen at the Plough sitting comfortably at the table, a pot of tea in front of her and her hair done up in rollers, discreetly covered by a scarf, ready for combing out for the evening's customers. Rudd accepted the offer of a cup of tea, chatted on other subjects and, eventually, led the conversation round to Mercer's house.

"It looks a big place for a man to run single-handed," he remarked.

"He's getting help," Ida said and launched into a long explanation of how a Mr. and Mrs. Blair, pensioners but still active, had agreed to go in daily, Mrs. Blair to do the cooking and cleaning, Mr. Blair to help in the garden, both of them leaving after lunch, as Mr. Mercer would get his own supper.

This led her into a long monologue about her own problems with daily help, namely the smiling deaf Dotty, who could be heard in the saloon bar, banging about as she tidied it up for the evening trade and singing "Abide with Me" in a lugubrious voice. Rudd commiserated with Ida but his thoughts were elsewhere. At least, the mornings should be safe for Mercer. That left the afternoons and the evenings to cover, and the nights. In fact, the greater part of the day. And for how long? For a fortnight? For a month? Rudd twitched his shoulders irritably. He was back to the old problem and it was not that much easier after all.

Ida was looking at the clock.

"Well," she said. "I suppose I'd better be getting myself ready for opening time."

She patted the rollers under the scarf and went out, calling loudly for her husband. A faint rumbling shout came from upstairs where George was having his afternoon's rest.

Rudd strolled round to the front of the pub and sat down on one of the benches. Now that the afternoon was drawing towards evening, the sunlight had a rich, golden fullness and the village looked utterly at peace. It was hard to imagine death in such a setting, or even danger.

Rudd stretched out his legs. He had long ago come to the conclusion that nothing was worthwhile that came too easily, and the only thing he dreaded was failure. If Mercer was killed . . .

He turned away from this line of thinking. Mercer would have to be protected. That was Rudd's job. In the meantime, the man had not yet arrived, the hut was empty and Rudd had the whole evening in front of him to enjoy, perhaps the last for some time in which he could relax and take life easily.

Mercer arrived, as expected, the next morning. Rudd walking deliberately past the house, saw the furniture van parked in the drive with Mercer's dark-green Rover drawn up behind it. There was no need for subterfuge this time. Several people were standing quite openly at the gate watching and Rudd joined them for a few minutes, listening to the comments as each piece of furniture was carried in. Then, amused, he walked on and, having made a circuit of the village by the lanes, he returned to the Plough in time for lunch.

It was another splendid day, hotter than ever, and for once Rudd did not fancy the heat and noise of the bar so, carrying his plate of beef salad and his pint of bitter, he escaped outside. He had only just settled himself at one of the tables when Mercer drove up, parked his car on the forecourt and went inside the pub. He emerged a few minutes later, also carrying a plate and a glass, noticed Rudd's presence for the first time and asked, with a smile, if he might join him.

Rudd nodded and moved up the bench to make room for him. Things were turning out well it seemed. He had hoped to get better acquainted with Mercer and here the man was, sitting down beside him and clearly ready to open a conversation.

"Nice pub," Mercer commented.

"Yes," said Rudd. "I'm very fond of it, and the landlord and his wife. I've been coming down here for years now."

"Oh?" said Mercer, interested. "You don't live in the village then?"

Rudd began his long-rehearsed story that had been practised before on people in the village and that gave the impression of his being a minor Civil Servant, with the additional information that he was staying longer this year on doctor's orders.

"Overwork," he explained.

Mercer seemed to accept the story without hesitation and did not question Rudd more closely on the exact nature of his work. And yet, the Inspector had the impression that he was very much on the alert. His eyes were watchful as well as interested and Rudd decided that he was a very shrewd and intelligent man, with a wide knowledge of human nature. He was certainly not a person to be fooled easily.

But Rudd too was experienced in handling people. He had also the advantage of having the kind of face that gave the impression of honesty and frankness; and Rudd set out deliberately to disarm Mercer.

"I hear you've just moved in," he remarked.

Mercer laughed. "I suppose news travels quickly in a village," he said.

"It's something you'll have to learn to live with," Rudd replied. "I'm country-bred myself and I know what it's like. It's usually harmless but people do take in interest in what's going on."

"So they may," Mercer replied, "but I've not found them all that forthcoming so far, apart from the landlord and his wife. I suppose I shall have to give them time."

"It may take years," Rudd said. "Country people don't make friends all that easily."

Mercer pulled a rueful face.

"I've been abroad a good deal over the past years," he explained, "and I'm afraid I'm not experienced in English village life. I was hoping to find a few like souls whom I could ask in for a drink or a game of bridge now and then."

He paused and Rudd had the feeling he was waiting for some reply. But what? Rudd drank some beer as he thought over both Mercer's remark and his motive for making it. It seemed that he was hoping Rudd would suggest some likely people. There was John Thurleigh, of course, and the vicar, and a retired doctor whom Rudd did not know very well.

But surely a man of Mercer's background would seek out his

own friends? Besides, Rudd could not imagine him finding loneliness irksome. He was too self-sufficient for that.

The moment passed. Mercer was looking at his watch.

"I'll have to get back," he said. "I left the removal men eating their sandwiches in the garden and I promised them I'd bring them some bottles of beer."

He went back into the Plough, leaving Rudd with the conclusion that he had read too much into Mercer's remark.

A few minutes later Mercer returned, carrying two quart bottles and, giving Rudd a casual wave of his hand, he got into the car and drove off.

Rudd watched him go, pleased with the encounter. It gave him the opportunity to get to know the man better. But the meeting had also had a disquieting effect on the Inspector. Now that he had seen Mercer at close quarters and talked to him, Rudd could see that he had a strong and positive personality and he could understand why Bravington had been anxious that Mercer was not to know that he was being protected. Once you got on the wrong side of him, he could be a ruthless and implacable enemy.

And what better way of getting on the good side of him than by making himself useful to him? If Mercer wanted to get acquainted with people in the village, then Rudd could easily introduce him to one or two who might have something in common with him. Thurleigh, for instance, although he was a solitary man, not much given to entertaining friends or visiting other people. But he was educated and his interest in books might form a common bond with Mercer.

All the same, the uneasiness persisted. He felt, for no reason that he could rationally explain, that instead of himself using Mercer, Mercer had in some subtle way manipulated him. It might be merely the effect that the man's personality had on his own, making the Inspector feel slightly at a disadvantage and ill at ease.

He puzzled over it as he stood at the bar, drinking his second pint of beer and then, impatient with his own thought, he dismissed it from his mind. But although he had banished it from his consciousness, it still went on troubling him.

That night he dreamed of the hut, only it was surrounded with bushes and trees, like the shrubbery in Mercer's garden. Someone was hiding among the dark branches but, in the inconsequential manner of dreams, it was Rudd himself who was in danger and the hidden presence among the leaves was Mercer's. He could not see him but he knew that he was there and the rustling movement in the darkness was full of unseen menace.

Rudd woke with a start. The rustling sound was there in reality and then, as full wakefulness returned, he realised that the sound he had heard was the night wind stirring the branches of the trees outside his window. It was only a dream but all the same, even when he switched on the bedside lamp, it remained with him and it was nearly an hour before the memory of it died down and he was able to get back to sleep again.

# 7

Rudd telephoned Bravington the next day, driving out to a public call box on the Fletchford road. Bravington sounded depressed when Rudd explained the difficulties of posting a man to keep watch on the hut.

"You'll have to cope with it as best you can, I suppose," he told the Inspector, as if he did not hold out much hope of it being properly done. But he cheered up at the news of Rudd's encounter with Mercer.

"That's excellent!" he cried. "Try to build up the contact. I know Mercer isn't the sort to take other people into his confidence. I'll leave it to you to make the best use of it you can."

Rudd saw little of Mercer in the next few days. Once or twice, as he passed in the car, Mercer lifted a hand in greeting but he did not appear again at the Plough and Rudd supposed he was still busy settling into the house. Ida passed on the information that Mrs. Blair had begun her duties and that the house was "lovely inside."

Meanwhile Rudd strolled about the village and the neighbouring countryside. But he paid only one more visit to the hut, borrowing George's field-glasses again. Yet even with these as an excuse for his presence near the river, he felt uneasy about going there too often. As it was, George teased him gently as he handed over the binoculars.

"I didn't know you were one for the birds," he commented, grinning. Rudd passed it off by replying lightly that he was thinking of taking it up as a hobby for his retirement, as it involved a lot of quiet sitting down. He did not, however, want it to become the subject of bar-room gossip and he would not put it past George to mention it in front of other people, just to raise a laugh.

He approached the hut warily as he had done before, listening and waiting to make sure it was empty before he stooped down beside the door and parted the thick, green leaves of the dock plant that hid the bottom hinge.

The wire was still in position. It had not been moved. As he pulled the leaves back into place and straightened up, he felt bewildered and baffled.

Someone had gone to a great deal of trouble to set up the place as a hide-out and yet had not used it for the past four days. Perhaps he intended to return. Perhaps the whole thing, the photographs, the typewritten note threatening Mercer's life, was merely an elaborate hoax, designed to frighten Mercer and nothing more. But if that was the intention it had singularly failed. Mercer showed no signs of fear; he did not seem to be showing even the elementary caution of a man who considered himself in danger.

No, it could not be a hoax. That was impossible. Nobody would go to the trouble of finding out Mercer's London address, or the fact that he was about to retire, unless he meant the threat seriously. The hut, too, was significant. The man intended to return. The question was: when?

Rudd stumped back to the village. The uneasiness he had felt was replaced now with the more positive emotion of anger. He had the suspicion that he was being fooled and he did not like it. Damn it all, surely something definite would have to happen soon! The days were passing, no move had yet been made and Rudd was beginning to feel the strain of being constantly on the watch. It was like tensing yourself for a blow to fall, without knowing when or where it would happen.

The first blow fell a few days later, delivered casually by Ida. She had been shopping and Rudd, returning from a prowl round the village that had produced nothing except an increased sense of baffled irritability, met her on her way back to the Plough and offered to carry her basket.

She talked for a few moments on trivial matters and then suddenly said, as if she had just remembered it,

"Have you heard about Mr. Mercer's car?"

Rudd knew instinctively that something important had occurred but he kept the excitement out of his voice as he replied,

"No. What's happened to it?"

"Someone took a pot-shot at it," Ida said with the triumphant air of one bringing interesting news.

"You mean, fired at it with a gun?" Rudd asked, trying to show no more than normal concern.

"Yes. With an air-rifle, so they say."

"An air-rifle?"

Rudd stopped in his tracks. Ida stopped too and looked at him so curiously that he was forced to pretend he had halted merely to scrape off a stone that had become stuck to the bottom of his shoe.

An air-rifle! It did not make sense. A revolver, yes; or a shot gun. But no-one making a serious attempt at murder would choose a short-range weapon of that sort. Even if used at close quarters, it would not necessarily be lethal.

Ida continued, "They were saying in the shop that it's done quite a bit of damage to the car door and he's taken it into the garage to have it fixed. I bet he's mad about it. I know I should be. People ought to be more careful, firing off guns without looking."

"I agree," said Rudd. He was surprised that Ida seemed to think so little of the incident until he remembered her country background. The possession of a gun, particularly an air-rifle, would seem perfectly normal.

"When did it happen?" he asked.

"That I couldn't tell you," she replied. "Yesterday, I think, Daisy Hood was telling me in the shop. She got it off Mrs. Blair; but you know what Daisy's like. She only takes in half what's told her and gets most of that wrong anyway."

They reached the pub and the subject was dropped. Rudd did not refer to it again but that afternoon he took his car along to the garage on the excuse that he wanted to check the oil and water.

Mercer's Rover was standing on the forecourt with Harry Kingston, the garage owner, squatting down beside it. As Rudd drove up, he stood up and walked towards him. Rudd refrained from mentioning Mercer's car until his own business at the garage had been settled, then he remarked casually, "I see you've got Mr. Mercer's car over there. I heard it got damaged."

"Got hit by an air-gun pellet," Kingston replied. He was a tall gangling man, never given to talking much.

"When did it happen?" Rudd asked, hoping Kingston would be able to supply the information that Ida had been unsure about.

"Yesterday afternoon, seemingly. He was driving along the Fletchford road when he felt something go ping against the side of the car. Said he didn't pay much attention at the time, thought it was a stone spun up off the wheels. It was only when he got into Fletchford that he noticed the damage.''

"I suppose it could have been dangerous," Rudd said hopefully. The incident was already beginning to fade into relative insignificance. Even Mercer had not paid much attention to it, it seemed.

Kingston looked doubtful.

"I suppose it could have been, if it'd hit him on the windscreen, say, and made him swerve. Mr. Mercer was more concerned about the damage to the car.''

They walked towards the Rover and round the back of it to the damaged side.

"Look at that," Kingston said. "Slap in the middle of the door panel. It's going to mean hammering it out and a respray.''

Rudd bent down to examine it more closely. The pellet had struck the rear passenger door on the driver's side but had not penetrated it. Even so, it had made a small, round but deep indentation from which the paint had flaked, leaving the raw metal exposed. A larger, more shallow depression surrounded it. Kingston ran his hand over it, with the concern of a good mechanic for the means of his trade.

"Any idea how it could have happened?" Rudd inquired. He felt he was asking too many questions. Kingston shrugged laconically.

"Probably kids in a field, taking a few pot-shots at birds. That's Mr. Mercer's opinion anyway. And he's not likely to trace them either. If they knew they'd hit a car, they're not going to own up.''

Rudd agreed and then moved away. It was time, he felt, to withdraw before Kingston became suspicious at his interest. Walking back to his car, he got in and drove off, taking the Fletchford road with the intention of telephoning Bravington with this new information. Then he changed his mind. There was really little to tell. Mercer's car had been hit by an air-gun pellet that might have been fired accidentally. That was hardly important. Or was it? It was difficult to tell if it had any significance or not. Like the incident in the basement garage, it could be simply a coincidence that had no real bearing on the case. On the other hand, perhaps he ought to go back to the hut to see if anyone had used it since his last visit. But the more often he went there the more likely he was to be seen.

For one of the rare occasions in his life, the Inspector was undecided what to do. In the end, he went back to his room at the Plough where he lay on the bed, staring up at the ceiling and trying to make some sense out of the situation.

As a child, he had played blind-man's buff, a game he hated, and he remembered the anger and bewilderment he had felt when, with his eyes blindfolded, he had groped about in the dark for the other children, heard their muffled laughter but could not reach them with his outstretched, clutching hands. He had taken refuge in sulking. And he realised that he was now reacting with the same kind of emotion, a to-hell-with-it attitude, an overwhelming desire to rind up Bravington and tell him he could keep his bloody case.

He heard George climb the stairs and go into the bedroom next door for his afternoon rest. The springs creaked as he climbed on to the bed and presently he started snoring. Downstairs, Ida was talking to Dotty in a high-pitched voice that went on and on.

There was not even any peace for him to think quietly and he sat up, put on his shoes and clumped angrily down the stairs.

The afternoon was fine but not even the weather, nor a long walk, dispelled his mood and he was returning, still in a grumpy frame of mind, at half past four, intending to call on John Thurleigh whom he had not seen for several days, in the hope that his company and conversation might take his mind off his own problems, when a voice called his name and, turning round, he saw Mercer walking towards him.

Rudd's mood brightened. The meeting with Mercer was a piece of good fortune in an otherwise bleak afternoon as far as action was concerned. He could now find out from Mercer more about the incident with the car and introduce him to Thurleigh which would give the Inspector a further contact with the man, although Rudd still had reservations about it and a vaguely uneasy conscience that he was using the schoolmaster to further his own ends. But he shrugged it off. He was doing Thurleigh no harm and possibly Mercer some good. The more people who came into contact with him, the more difficult it would be for Mercer's killer to attack him.

"I'm calling on an acquaintance," Rudd said, as Mercer fell into step beside him. "I don't know if you'd care to come along and meet him."

"I'd be delighted," Mercer replied.

Rudd gave him a sly sideways look. Certainly, the man did not seem in any way affected by his recent experience. If anything, he was more brisk and buoyant than ever, his good-looking, craggy face alive with interest and his voice a shade more self-confident than usual.

"Who is this person we're meeting?" he asked.

"His name's John Thurleigh," Rudd replied. "He teaches

history. He's rather a quiet man and I don't think he mixes much in the village, although he and the vicar have a game of chess together occasionally. I think you'll like him.''

Mercer did not reply and after an awkward silence, in which Rudd felt slightly gauche, like a schoolboy trying to get on good terms with a prefect, the Inspector cleared his throat and said,

"I heard you'd had some trouble with your car."

Mercer laughed.

"Oh that!" was all he said in reply. "Yes, a blasted nuisance it is too. I shall be without a car until Kingston puts it right."

There seemed to be nothing more to say on the subject. Mercer had effectively dismissed it as something trivial and not worth further discussion and Rudd felt again the baffled anger that had risen in him when he found the wire on the hut door untouched. Only this time it was directed at Mercer himself, the potential victim. It seemed to the Inspector that he was being subjected to total uncooperation on every side.

They walked up the path to Thurleigh's front door, Rudd knocking more energetically on it than he intended, and it was opened by the schoolmaster, blinking a little in the dim light of the passage after the brilliant sunshine of the back garden where he had been working.

"Oh, it's you," he said, recognising Rudd. "This is nice. Do come in."

Although Rudd had often asked Thurleigh to call him by his Christian name, some natural reticence on Thurleigh's part prevented him from doing this and, as "Mr. Rudd" would have sounded too formal after their long acquaintance, he now called Rudd nothing at all, if he could avoid addressing him directly. Rudd, however, with more directness, always called him John.

"I hope you don't mind but I've brought someone along to meet you," the Inspector said. "It's . . ."

He paused for a second and Mercer, with no inhibiting diffidence, took over the introduction.

"I'm Alec Mercer," he announced, holding out his hand. "I've bought the Threadgolds' house in Tiler's Lane. I've been hoping to get to know a few people in the village."

As Rudd had feared, Thurleigh was immediately flustered. He had been gardening and he hesitated to shake hands as his own were dirt-soiled. Rubbing one on his trousers, he offered it apologetically and then at the last moment almost withdrew it.

Rudd watched with a feeling of sadness and affection. Beside

Mercer, Thurleigh cut a poor figure with his shyness and awkward-
ness and yet, of the two, Rudd felt more drawn towards him. He
was a gentle, genuine person and the Inspector valued his friendship
for these very reasons.

"Delighted," Thurleigh was murmuring. "Do come inside."

They entered the narrow hall, Mercer seeming to take up most
of the space, not just physically but also with the force of his
personality. Thurleigh, apologising, limped ahead of them into the
pleasant, cluttered sitting-room.

"Sit down," he was saying, lunging awkwardly forward to
move books off chairs. "I'll make some tea."

He seemed glad of an excuse to get out of the room.

Rudd sat down and watched Mercer who, thoroughly at ease,
walked about and examined the titles of the books in the crammed
shelves.

"Your friend, John Thurleigh, seems a great reader," he commented.

Rudd, for some obscure reason, felt resentful at the remark. He
could not explain why but the sight of Mercer strolling about, his
hands in his pockets and a slightly amused smile on his face,
irritated him. Perhaps Thurleigh's lack of ease had put Rudd on the
defensive for his sake.

"Yes," was all he said in reply.

Mercer halted in front of a photograph that stood on top of the
bureau.

"Thurleigh's wife?" he asked.

"Yes. She died three years ago," Rudd answered.

"I see," Mercer replied. He examined the photograph for a few
seconds but did not attempt to touch it, which pleased Rudd. At least
the man, for all his self-assurance, had that much sensitivity.

Thurleigh returned at this moment, carrying a tray of tea-things.
He had washed his hands and tidied up his appearance and seemed
also to have regained a little of his composure.

They had tea. Thurleigh asked Mercer a few polite questions
about himself which Mercer answered in a friendly manner. Rudd
drank his tea and let the two men talk. Mercer seemed to be more
subdued, as if he was aware that his ebullient performance on first
meeting Thurleigh had been too overwhelming.

Performance.

As the word came into his mind, it brought him up sharply. But
he was right. There had been something false about the bonhomie

that Mercer had displayed. It was as if he was acting the part of the cheerful neighbour, eager to be on friendly terms.

Rudd sipped his tea and watched him with quickened interest. He wondered what the real man was like. Was it the one who was now sitting relaxed and easy, discussing books with Thurleigh?

Anyway, Thurleigh was evidently taken in. His thin face was eager and flushed with pleasure. His eyes had lost their habitual anxious expression and he was leaning forward in his chair, replying to some remark that Mercer had made.

"Oh, I do so agree with you," he was saying.

Agree to what? Rudd had not been following the conversation, absorbed as he was in Mercer's personality and his own reaction to it.

A small seed of dislike for the man that he had felt before began to take on a more positive form. It puzzled Rudd. There was, on the surface, nothing about him that could cause antipathy. He was charming, courteous, pleasant to speak to, intelligent, an interesting personality, and yet Rudd could not like him. He tried to analyse his feelings.

The fact of the matter was, the man was bogus but not in any obvious sense of the word. Mercer was far too clever to act any part in other than a first-rate manner. He was a sham in the way that some good actors are shams, who have become so used to playing other people that their own personalities have become absorbed into the fictional characters they have created. As an agent, Mercer too must have played many roles. Perhaps this was why Rudd sensed the same sham quality about him. It did not, of course, make any difference to the investigation. Mercer had to be protected whatever the Inspector's personal feelings about him might be. But it gave another dimension to the case.

In effect, Rudd was himself playing a part, that of a holiday-maker who happened to be staying in the village, knowing nothing of Mercer or his past. Added to this, he would now have to dissemble friendship, or at least hide his antipathy, and Rudd had the feeling that this was not going to be easy. Mercer was no fool. Bogus he might be but he was also sensitive. He could not have survived in Nazi-occupied France if he had not had a sixth sense about people. It was going to be more tricky than the Inspector had bargained for. Not that he minded. He preferred a case that was a challenge and not merely routine. And in this case he was certainly going to be stretched, for he had not only Mercer's personality to deal with but the equally devious and intelligent man who threatened

Mercer's life. He was no fool, either. But if Rudd was up against it, Mercer was too.

It crossed Rudd's mind that Mercer might have refused Bravington's help out of a kind of intellectual superiority. He might very well consider that no-one could get the better of him and that he was more than capable of dealing with the man himself. If this was so, then it was a dangerous assumption. Whoever threatened him had so far won every trick; he had managed to get into the village unseen and set up his hide-out in the hut . . .

"You're looking very serious."

Mercer's comment interrupted his train of thought. Glancing up, Rudd found his eyes on him, amused and knowing, as if he had read the Inspector's thoughts.

But that, of course, was ridiculous, he told himself. All the same, he felt very vulnerable under that bright, sharp gaze and he wondered if he had not, in his reverie, unwittingly let some expression cross his face that might have indicated to Mercer his feelings about him.

"Just trying to follow your conversation," he replied, letting his features relax into his frank countryman's look. He even managed a slight chuckle. "A bit above my head most of the time, I'm afraid."

"You're being too modest," Thurleigh said gently. "You play a good game of chess, as I know to my cost."

So that's what they've been talking about, Rudd thought. They must have moved away from the subject of books. He wondered if Mercer had noticed the mistake but he did not appear to have done so. He was getting to his feet as if ready to go.

"I'd be delighted if you'd give me a game one evening," he said to Thurleigh.

"I'd enjoy that," Thurleigh replied. He sounded genuinely pleased at the invitation and Rudd felt a surge of emotion that he could not define. It was not exactly jealousy. It did not really matter to him that Mercer and Thurleigh might become friends. It was subtler than that; a kind of protective anxiety towards the schoolmaster for being too trusting and for not seeing Mercer as Rudd saw him.

Yet, as they left the house and walked up the road together, Mercer remarked,

"I liked John Thurleigh very much."

It was said with what seemed real warmth and Rudd wondered if perhaps, after all, he had been wrong in his judgement of the man.

# 8

Rudd saw nothing of Mercer for two days and then one morning, unexpectedly, he telephoned him at the Plough and asked him to his house that evening for a drink. Rudd accepted with alacrity. He wanted to keep up the acquaintanceship with him and the invitation meant that he would get a good idea of the lay-out of the house and its surroundings.

However, later Rudd began to wish that Mercer had chosen another evening. The weather forecast that morning had said "Rain spreading from the west." What it had not forecast was the force with which it would fall. Eating alone in the little dining-room, Rudd watched it pounding on the gravel forecourt outside the window, running down the slope to join the stream of water that filled the gutters at the side of the road. He would get soaked just getting the car out to drive to Mercer's.

George lent him a macintosh and, with that over his shoulders, he dashed across the yard to the barn. It had grown so dark that he was forced to switch on the headlights as he drove through the village, deserted in the rain, not a person out of doors.

Perhaps in anticipation of his arrival, Mercer had switched on the porch light and, as Rudd ducked out of the car and ran up the steps to ring the bell, he answered it almost immediately.

"Filthy weather," he remarked.

Rudd, following him inside, agreed. Having hung up the borrowed raincoat to dry, Mercer led the way across the hall to a door at the back that led, the Inspector guessed, from his own brief survey of the house, to the long drawing-room at the far end.

"I thought we'd use this room," Mercer was saying. "The

small study's cosier but I'm afraid the wiring in there isn't finished yet.''

The drawing-room was furnished simply but expensively with two huge, black leather sofas, placed either side of the fireplace, in which a log fire was burning to dispel the damp chill of the evening. Apart from a coffee-table of white marble, a few rugs on the floor and a huge antique tallboy of figured walnut that stood against the inner wall, the room was empty. Rudd liked the severe masculine simplicity and comfort, the absence of clutter.

''Whisky?'' Mercer asked, going to the tallboy and opening the doors of the upper section. Rudd saw that the interior had been fitted out as a drinks cabinet with shelves for glasses and a compartment to hold bottles.

Rudd watched him speculatively as he poured the drinks. There was something edgy in Mercer's behaviour that the Inspector had never seen in him before, a tension in his shoulders and the way he carried his head, and he wondered if, for all his apparent unconcern over the threat against his life, he did not, after all, take it more seriously than he pretended.

And then, as if Mercer were in some curious way aware of Rudd's thoughts, he said, as he handed the Inspector his drink and sat down opposite him on the other sofa,

''I can't settle down this evening. I've been in the house all afternoon because of this damned rain and it's beginning to get me down. I'm used to the sun.''

''You've lived abroad, haven't you?'' Rudd asked. It was safe to say this. Mercer himself had given him this information.

''Yes, mostly the Middle East. At least, for the past few years.''

Rudd could not resist asking, ''Oh really? What were you doing out there?''

He was sitting a little primly on the sofa, like a guest not quite at ease, but behind the polite facade, he was very watchful and alert.

''Business,'' Mercer replied. ''I had a small export firm, dealing mainly in local products, leather goods, silver, hand-woven rugs, that sort of thing.''

''Interesting, I should imagine,'' Rudd remarked.

''It took me into the villages quite a lot,'' Mercer said. ''It involved travelling.''

As a cover for an agent, Rudd could see that a business of that kind would be very useful.

The conversation turned to more general topics. More drinks

were poured, the fire burned up, warming the room, Mercer became more expansive. He was a good raconteur and Rudd, relaxed, listened appreciatively. The man was certainly excellent company.

It was about ten o'clock that they heard the crash from the adjoining room. Mercer was standing in front of the open cabinet, refilling their glasses, when it happened. He turned immediately and Rudd, every policeman's nerve in his body alert, sat up and looked in the direction of the noise.

"What the bloody hell's that?" Mercer cried and made at once for the door, Rudd following closely behind him. In the hall, Mercer flung open the door of the adjoining room and fumbled at the wall for the electric-light switch. Rudd heard it click but no lights came on. Mercer cursed again and Rudd heard him mutter something about the "bloody wiring." Then he pushed past the Inspector, ran back into the sitting-room and came out again seconds later carrying a heavy torch in one hand and a revolver in the other.

Rudd, left alone for those few seconds in the open doorway, had little time in which to register anything. The confusion of the moment, Mercer's precipitate action in flinging past him, throwing him off balance, had startled him. He could see nothing of the room beyond. It was in total darkness, except for a pale rectangle that indicated the position of the pair of French windows leading out into the garden at the back of the house. A draught of cold, damp air suggested that they were open.

He had barely time to take this in when Mercer returned with the torch which he switched on, playing its beam about the room. Even then, Rudd had only brief glimpses of its interior. The torch-light picked out momentarily a desk against the far wall, a fireplace next to it, then the French windows, one leaf of which was standing open, and then, on the other side of the room, a lamp lying on the floor, its china base shattered. It had evidently been standing on top of a set of bookshelves that ran the length of the room. The beam of light played across them for a few seconds, glittering for a moment on silver.

The next instant, Mercer was striding across the room and, shouting to Rudd to follow him, had plunged out through the open window into the rain and the darkness, the torch waving wildly to and fro. Rudd followed him. He was not familiar enough with the garden from the one visit he had paid to it on the afternoon before Mercer's arrival to the village and he had forgotten that the terrace was on a different level to the lawn. He stumbled on the steps, almost fell and only saved himself by clutching at an ornamental stone vase that crowned the top of the wall. The shock brought him up short and he stood quite still, looking about him, trying to get his eyes used to the darkness.

The rain was still falling heavily and a strong wind was now blowing, giving an impression of noise and confusion, of threshing branches and hissing rain, of dim clouds tearing past overhead and of the light from Mercer's torch blowing about too, it seemed, and flashing on the far side of the lawn.

It suddenly occurred to Rudd what danger Mercer was in, even though he was armed. The light of the torch made him an easy target. Anyone concealed behind one of the bushes could pick him off as easily as a rabbit caught in the headlights of a car.

He was about to shout a warning when the light came bobbing back across the lawn. Mercer was returning.

"Not a damned sight of anyone," he said. He was breathing heavily. "Whoever it was must have made off."

He went quickly back into the house through the French windows and, a second or two later, when Rudd followed him into the room, Mercer was switching on an angle-poise lamp that stood on the desk.

"Well," he said, "it doesn't look as if he had time to take anything."

Rudd could now see the room clearly for the first time. He noticed the pool of water on the parquet flooring where the rain had driven in through the open window and the display of silver objects on top of the bookshelves that he had only glimpsed before. They were mostly salvers and plates, a few flagons and bowls, richly chased and engraved.

"You think he was after the silver?" Rudd asked.

If Mercer was going to explain away the incident as an attempted burglary than he would have to go along with it.

Mercer said, "It seems likely, doesn't it? He's probably been snooping around here when I've been out, noticed the silver and thought he'd help himself. Ironically, it's not all that valuable; bazaar stuff mostly that I picked up in the Middle East but I wouldn't like to lose it. If he hadn't knocked that lamp down, he might have got away with it, too."

"The French windows were locked?" Rudd asked.

He found himself in a difficult position. As a policeman, his instinct and training made him want to take over the investigation but he knew he could do no such thing. Mercer would immediately suspect him. Rudd could show only the kind of knowledge that an ordinary citizen might be expected to have.

"I'd locked them but they weren't bolted," Mercer replied, walking over and opening back one leaf while Rudd longed to shout, "Fingerprints!"

"Look here," Mercer added. "This is how he got in."

He was pointing to the outside of the door. Rudd joined him and examined it. The wood had been splintered where the lock had been forced open. He guessed a jemmy had been used, or possibly a nail bar. It had certainly been effective in shattering the lock. Yet they had heard nothing until the lamp was knocked over. On further reflection, Rudd did not think this significant. Because of the weather, the windows were shut and the curtains drawn in the sitting-room. Besides, the house seemed to be solidly constructed with thick walls. If the man had levered the door open with care the only noise would have been the slight cracking sound made as the wood splintered and the metal tongue of the lock was forced out of position. It was not surprising that it had been inaudible in the next room, especially as the wind had risen and the noise of it would have given effective cover.

"I think you ought to phone the police," Rudd said, coming quickly to a decision.

Mercer looked doubtful.

"Do you think it's necessary? What good are they going to do? Nothing's been taken and quite obviously the man's got clean away. And tracker dogs are going to be useless in this rain."

"All the same, I think they ought to be told," Rudd replied firmly.

Mercer shrugged.

"Perhaps you're right. Would you mind ringing them while I clear up some of the mess in here? The phone's in the hall."

It was on the tip of Rudd's tongue to reply that nothing ought to be touched until the police had examined the room but he stopped himself in time. In the doorway, he paused to look back. Mercer was in the act of closing and bolting the French windows, stepping with fastidious care over the pool of water on the parquet floor.

Rudd quietly closed the door and went into the hall where he telephoned the police, giving them the details of the incident. As he was speaking, he could hear Mercer moving about inside the room. He came out just as Rudd was replacing the receiver.

"They're sending a police car over straightaway," Rudd announced.

"Right," Mercer said without much interest. He seemed bored now with the whole affair. "Well, I suggest we go back into the drawing-room and have a drink in comfort before they arrive."

In the drawing-room Mercer went over to the cabinet and poured two whiskies but, before he did so, he opened one of the drawers in the lower section, putting into it the revolver and the torch which he had been carrying in his pockets. There was nothing furtive about this. He made no attempt to cover up his movements and Rudd felt justified in asking, "Was it loaded?"

"The gun, you mean?" asked Mercer. He laughed. "Yes, as a matter of fact it was. I got into the habit of keeping a loaded revolver handy when I was in the Middle East. Particularly when my business took me into the villages."

"Would you have used it?" Rudd asked. He hoped the question showed no more than an understandable curiosity.

"Tonight? I don't know. I hadn't really thought about it," Mercer replied.

"It was more of a natural reflex to pick it up. I suppose if I'd caught the man in the room I would have threatened him with it and possibly shot him somewhere harmless, in the leg for instance, if he'd shown any resistance."

It was said in a curiously off-hand manner that surprised and, at the same time, slightly shocked Rudd. Although he had some knowledge of the use of fire-arms through his police training, he had never carried or used a gun and for Mercer, an ordinary citizen, to talk of shooting someone, even in the leg, struck him as cold-blooded. But then, Rudd realised, Mercer was not an ordinary citizen. As an agent, he would be familiar with guns and had probably fired one on more than one occasion.

Mercer shut the drawer and carried the glass of whisky over to the sofa where Rudd was sitting. He stood over him, offering the glass and looking down at him with an amused expression on his face.

"You look worried," he said.

"I am worried," Rudd confessed.

And so ought *you* to be, was the Inspector's silent comment.

"There's no need to be," Mercer replied lightly. "I don't think it's likely he'll try again. I should imagine we've frightened him off for good."

"All the same . . ." Rudd began.

"All the same," Mercer echoed with a faint touch of irony in his voice, "I shall take a few precautions against this kind of thing happening again. I'll get a stronger lock put on those French windows and, as I'm off to London tomorrow for a few days, I suppose I'd better not leave the silver out but get it locked up in the house.''

Rudd drank his whisky without speaking. The old feeling of baffled anger returned. He was caught in an impossible situation, knowing more than he dared reveal. He could not tell the police what he knew. Nor could he warn Mercer of the real danger he was in.

Mercer's attitude too added to his sense of frustration. He seemed no more concerned over the incident than one would expect him to be if it had indeed been only an attempted burglary. He must have an iron nerve, Rudd thought to himself and then it occurred to him that this was the very quality the man did in fact possess. He had lived and worked for months in that hotel in France during the war as a British agent and yet had kept up the pretence in front of the German officers. It had been a dangerous and elaborate game which could have cost him his life. It was natural for him not to show fear.

"I'm bloody annoyed about the lamp," Mercer was saying. "The base of it was a rather nice porcelain vase."

"Valuable?" Rudd asked automatically. He was thinking that if Mercer intended going to London for a few days, his own task of keeping guard over the man would be considerably lightened. It would be Bravington's problem and Rudd would welcome a few days' rest. Even if Mercer was showing no signs of strain, the Inspector was certainly beginning to feel it himself.

Mercer made some reply about the vase that Rudd did not listen to properly. He was thinking that he would certainly now have to telephone Bravington. The incident that evening was far more serious than the business with the air-gun pellet or the car in the basement garage.

But as he thought it, it suddenly struck him that this affair could just as easily be explained away. An attempted burglary was perfectly feasible and again he was faced with the problem of deciding just how significant it really was. Was it an attempt on Mercer's life? If it was, it had been badly bungled. And for someone who had waited years to take his revenge, it seemed a clumsy way of going about it.

"Oh blast it!" Rudd said aloud. So busy had he been with his thoughts, that he had not been paying attention to the glass of whisky that he held in his hand and some of the spirit had splashed

ver his trousers. As he scrubbed at it with his handkerchief, Mercer
aid,

"We both seem to be rather damp, one way and another.
Vould you like a change of clothes? I could rig you up with some
ry trousers and a shirt."

Rudd felt his jacket. Although he had followed Mercer into the
arden, he had not been out long enough to have got really wet.
Jow that Mercer had called his attention to it, he could see now that
he man's thin cashmere sweater and twill trousers were soaked
hrough.

"I'll be all right," he admitted. "I didn't get all that wet. I
hink you ought to get changed, though. When the police come,
hey're bound to question you for some time. You could easily catch
a cold."

"You're probably right," Mercer admitted. "In that case, if
ou really don't want to borrow some dry things, I'll leave you
lown here and get changed myself. Help yourself to more whisky if
ou want it."

He left the room and Rudd returned to his thoughts. The
accident with the whisky and his own burst of verbal anger had
cleared his mind. It suddenly occurred to him that there could be
another explanation of the incidents.

They had been deliberately planned with the object of wearing
lown Mercer's nerves and perhaps they were, for all Mercer's
apparent coolness, already beginning to succeed. He remembered
now how edgy the man had been on Rudd's arrival. If this was so, it
was a cruel and subtle way of taking revenge; not the quick and
merciful coup de grâce that Rudd had been expecting, the bullet
fired to kill; but a drawn-out game, like a cat playing with a mouse,
extending the agony until the victim is reduced to a helpless mass of
nerves, crouched shivering in a corner, almost welcoming death as a
release. Someone must hate Mercer very much to go to all this
trouble, Rudd thought, and he felt a sudden pity for the man that
overrode his previous antipathy towards him.

The idea, too, that the revenge against Mercer might take this
long-term form upset the Inspector's former ideas about the case. It
might take weeks, perhaps months, before Mercer's enemy eventually showed his hand and delivered the final blow. It was a long
revenge, indeed; a very long time in the planning of it and possibly a
long time in its execution. It occurred to him that Mercer might
crack and himself ask for protection. But how long would it be
before his pride would allow him to do this? Rudd considered this

carefully. He did not know Mercer well enough to judge this, although Bravington might have a better knowledge of his character.

This thought led him on to wonder if the man who sought Mercer's life might not also know him; not just as a supposed German collaborator, standing on a French railway platform all those years ago, arranging for a train-load of prisoners to be sent to their death, someone that had followed him at a distance over the years; but much more intimately than this.

Rudd sat upright.

In that case, the photograph was simply a blind, to put Mercer off the scent and to lead him away from the person's real identity; someone who, if Rudd's surmise was correct, had been close to him, perhaps in daily contact; an employee, say, at the hotel where Mercer had worked and who had suffered or whose family had suffered at the hands of the Germans and who blamed Mercer for what had happened. It made better sense. Rudd could imagine someone watching Mercer day after day, studying him like a specimen under the microscope, learning his strengths and his weaknesses, planning how, later on, he could bring this man to his knees.

The sound of a car drawing up outside the house interrupted his thoughts. A door slammed, someone rang the bell and a moment later Rudd heard voices in the hall. The police had evidently arrived.

Rudd relaxed and lay back in his seat, stretching out his legs towards the log fire. He felt more at ease at that moment than he had for several days now that he had reached a better understanding of the case and, although it was by no means over, he thought it would be less complicated from now on. Several pieces of the puzzle had dropped into place and he felt optimistic that it would not be long before he had the whole picture.

About a quarter of an hour later Mercer entered the room, looking tired and strained as if the evening had suddenly become too much for him.

"I suppose you heard the police arrive," he said to Rudd. "They'd like to speak to you."

Rudd got to his feet and left the room.

A police inspector and a sergeant were waiting in the study, the Inspector seated at the desk with a notebook open in front of him, while the sergeant stood by the French windows, closed now with the curtains drawn over them. Rudd noticed also that the broken fragments of the vase had been picked up and were now lying on top of the bookshelves although the lamp-fitting and the shade were still on the floor. The pool of water that had been lying on the floor in front of the window had also been cleared up and a mass of damp and crumpled newspaper was stuffed in the waste-paper basket.

Rudd inwardly sighed. If he had been in charge of the investigation he would have had a few sharp words to say to Mercer about the need to touch nothing at the scene of the crime.

The inspector, a tall, thin-faced man, introduced himself as Moffat and asked Rudd to be seated. It was a new experience for Rudd to be on the receiving end of a police inquiry and, as he sat down, he deliberately assumed a slightly tense attitude and expression such as an ordinary citizen might be expected to show when faced with the unusual situation of giving evidence, for he realised that he must not give away, either directly or indirectly, his own connection with the police force.

But the interview was brief. He was asked his name and his present and his permanent address, and then he was invited to give his account of the evening's incident. There was, after all, little that he could tell and it was clear from the rather perfunctory questions put to him that Moffat considered he had already got all the details he was likely to obtain from his earlier interview with Mercer. Rudd merely described how they had heard the crash of the falling lamp and how he had followed Mercer to the threshold of the darkened room.

Moffat interrupted him at this point to ask,

"So you saw nobody, Mr. Rudd?"

Rudd replied that this was so, wondering as he did so whether Mercer had admitted going back to the drawing-room to fetch the revolver. But in fact the question never arose. Moffat moved on to Mercer's search of the garden and Rudd explained that he had stood on the terrace just outside the French windows but had not followed Mercer any further.

"Do you think you may be able to trace the man?" Rudd could not resist asking, and saw the smile come over Moffat's face that Rudd himself had often used when interviewing a witness who asked a question, however innocuous: a polite, friendly and totally non-committal smile.

"We'll certainly do our best," Moffat replied, which was exactly what Rudd himself would have said under similar circumstances.

The interview was over. Moffat closed his notebook, thanked Rudd for his cooperation and explained that he might be needed at some time to sign an official statement.

Rudd returned to the drawing-room where he found Mercer

standing with his back to the fire, another glass of whisky in his hand. He offered Rudd a drink but he refused. He was anxious now to get out of the house as soon as possible.

Mercer accompanied him into the hall.

"I'm sorry you got mixed up in this business," Mercer said, as Rudd put on the raincoat he had borrowed from George.

"Not at all," Rudd replied disarmingly. "I rather enjoyed it. It made for a bit of excitement in an otherwise quiet holiday. I believe you said you were going to London?" he added. "When will you be back? I'd like to ask you to the Plough one evening for a drink with me."

As he had hoped, Mercer took the question as perfectly natural.

"I'm off tomorrow, by train as the car's still being fixed up. I should be back by Saturday."

"I'll be in touch with you sometime after that, then," Rudd replied.

Mercer let him out of the house but to the Inspector's relief returned indoors immediately, closing the door behind him. Rudd did not want to run the risk of the man noticing that, as he drove off, he turned left along Tiler's Lane in the direction that led away from the village and towards the farm.

Having parked the car at the side of the entrance drive to the farm a little distance from the buildings, he got out and, taking a torch that he always kept in the glove compartment, he began to walk along the causeway towards the river.

The rain had stopped but a damp wind was blowing. Overhead the clouds had broken, revealing a round, pale moon that seemed to be racing across the sky as the clouds tore past. He could hear the reeds hissing in the irrigation ditches and presently, as he climbed the slope to the top of the dyke, the sound of the river running between the banks. It was high tide and the black water ran swiftly, streaked and pitted with flecks of moonlight.

The path along the top of the sea-wall was slippery with wet clay and grass. Rudd trod carefully for this reason and not because he suspected that the hut was occupied. He was, in fact, convinced that it would be empty. Mercer's killer, he realised now, had no further need of it. He had probably used it only in the first few days when he was getting to know the village and its lay-out, possibly before Mercer's arrival. Once he was familiar with the district, he could act from a distance, staying at some hotel, perhaps in Ipswich, perhaps in London even, returning to the village only when he needed.

He had probably found a good hiding-place for a car, even though Rudd had at first discounted this possibility. Or he might use a motor-bike. It would be easier to hide. All he would have to do was to park it somewhere out of sight and yet within walking distance of Mercer's house. That was what Rudd was now convinced had happened that evening.

The incident with the air-rifle took a little more explaining but it was still a feasible proposition. The man must have known that, sooner or later, Mercer would drive into Fletchford and he had simply waited in a field near the side of the road for his car to appear. It took patience, but then he was a very patient man. He had waited thirty years to take his revenge. What was a mere few days on that time scale?

Rudd reached the hut and scrambled down the slope. Stooping down, he parted the wet dock leaves. The tiny thread of wire across the hinge gleamed copper in the light of his torch. So he had been right. The hut had not been used and, satisfied, he made his way back along the causeway to the car.

The Plough was in darkness when he returned but the back door had been left open for him and, having bolted it behind him, he tip-toed upstairs to the bedroom and switched on the light. He could see now that his shoes and the bottoms of his trouser legs were wet through and caked with clay, and he left them lying on the floor to be dealt with in the morning.

In the morning, too, he must telephone Bravington and find out if it would be possible for him to arrange for Rudd to make a trip to France. With Mercer away in London until Saturday, it seemed a good opportunity to make a few inquiries in the town where Mercer had been placed as an agent during the war.

For Rudd was now convinced that the answer to the secret lay there. There must be someone still left alive who knew Mercer in those days and who could throw some light on the identity of the man who was seeking his life; a man who, if Rudd's new line of reasoning was correct, had been close to Mercer in those war years and who had a strong personal motive for wishing him dead.

# 9

Rudd made a point the following morning of telling George and Ida of the attempted break-in at Mercer's house. There was no reason not to do so. It was hardly secret, for the Blairs, who went in daily to help Mercer with domestic cleaning and gardening, would surely be told something of what had happened, if only to explain away the shattered lock on the French windows in the study. Besides, by passing on the information, Rudd was hoping for some return in the way of gossip in the Plough or about the village. Someone might have noticed a car parked in some hidden place at the time of the incident, although the Inspector held out no great hopes for this. The heavy rain the previous evening must have kept most people indoors. However, it was a chance not to be overlooked.

Dotty bore the muddy trousers and shoes off for cleaning, Rudd explaining that they had got in that condition when he helped search Mercer's garden for the intruder.

Later that morning he drove out of the village and telephoned Bravington from a public call box. Bravington listened in silence while the Inspector gave as brief an account as he could of the incident and the fresh conclusions he had reached about the indentity of Mercer's attacker.

"Someone who was close to him; possibly worked with him?" Bravington said thoughtfully. "It certainly makes sense."

"That's why I want to go to Demour," Rudd went on. "Mercer's going to be in London until Saturday, so I could spend at least two days making inquiries that end. Could it be arranged?"

"Yes, of course," Bravington replied. "Leave it to me. It'll take several hours but I'll get it pushed through as fast as possible.

Look Rudd, I'll meet you for dinner tonight. Do you know Essingham? It's a village about ten miles from Barnston, off the main Ipswich road. There's a hotel there that serves very good food. It's called the Fox. I'll meet you there at eight o'clock tonight. Now, you're going to need an excuse for being away from the Plough for a couple of days. I'll get someone at the office to telephone you. You have a sister haven't you?''

"That's right," Rudd replied, thinking that it was sharp of Bravington to have remembered this piece of information.

"Don't be surprised then if your 'sister' gets in touch with you sometime today," Bravington continued with a note of unexpected amusement in his voice.

"What about Mercer?" Rudd asked.

"Don't worry about him," Bravington replied. "If he's in London, he's our problem. I'll see that he's protected."

"I'd like a photograph of Mercer taken at the time he was in Demour," Rudd said. "Something I can show to the people while I'm over there."

"That'll be arranged," Bravington promised.

Rudd rang off and returned to the Plough where he spent the rest of the morning sitting in the garden, reading and waiting for the promised telephone call. He had already told Ida that he would be out for supper that evening as he was meeting a friend.

The telephone call came at lunchtime. Rudd was in the bar when the phone rang and George, having answered it, passed the receiver to the Inspector, saying,

"It's for you."

Rudd took it.

"Hello?" said an unknown woman's voice. "Is that you dear? I'm sorry to phone up and spoil your holiday but there's been some trouble with the builders over the new garage and I really feel you ought to be here to sort it out."

Rudd kept his face straight for George's benefit, who was standing close by at the bar, wiping down the counter and, Rudd was sure, listening in to the conversation at the same time.

"That's all right, Dorothy," he replied. He was thoroughly enjoying the situation. "Don't worry about it. I'll come home and stay for a few days and get it sorted out. It can't be today, I'm afraid. I'm meeting a friend this evening and I can't get in touch with him to put him off. I'll make it tomorrow."

He couldn't resist adding,

"How's the dog? Is he missing me?"

"He sits by the door waiting for you to come home and take him for a lovely long walkies," replied the woman, joining in the spirit of the occasion.

"Give him a pat for me," Rudd replied and rang off, turning to George, his expression deliberately a little worried.

"Trouble?" George asked solicitously.

"Not really," Rudd replied. "It's my sister. She gets a bit fussed at times. We've got the builders in and evidently some problem's turned up. I'd better get down there tomorrow and sort it out. I shouldn't be away for more than a couple of days. You'll keep my room for me?"

"Of course," said George and added, man to man, "Women! There's always something they'll find to make a fuss about."

It was said for Ida's benefit who was serving at the bar and she rose to the bait, as George knew she would, and tossed her head indignantly, making her long ear-rings swing.

Later that evening Rudd drove over to Essingham. It was one of those consciously picturesque villages, photographs of which appear on calendars illustrating the beauties of the English countryside. Thatched and plastered cottages, with decorative bands of pargeting, a Norman church and a row of medieval almshouses made it look, Rudd thought, like a film set; while the Fox might have been designed for the tourist trade. The fact that it was genuinely Elizabethan, that the old beams and bricks of its facade, its mullioned windows and steep roof of weathered tiles were not faked, did not prevent Rudd from regarding it with a faint sneer as he parked the car.

The interior was, as he had imagined, full of oak panelling and a lot of brass and pewter in the shape of warming pans and tankards and hunting horns. The service, he guessed, would be supercilious, and the food, despite what Bravington had said, indifferent but expensive. There he was wrong. Bravington was already in the dining-room, and as each course was served, Rudd was surprised and delighted at the excellence of it.

They talked quietly as they ate. Bravington wanted to know in more detail what had happened and Rudd re-told the two incidents.

"So you think he might take his time?" Bravington asked, looking grave.

"That's my opinion," Rudd replied, lingering over his home-made game *pâté*, savouring every morsel of it. "I don't think he's in any hurry to get rid of Mercer. As I said to you on the phone, I see it as a form of slow psychological torture."

Bravington wiped his lips on his napkin. His austere face looked bleaker than ever.

"It would make sense if the man we're looking for had a similar experience himself; was captured by the Germans and tortured. Or had a relative or a close friend who suffered in the same way," he said.

"And blamed Mercer for it," Rudd added. "He was acting the part of a German collaborator. Someone may have suspected him of betrayal. I must admit that business with the photograph of the train-load of prisoners didn't ring true at the time. It was too anonymous. Why should someone pick on Mercer because a train-load of prisoners gets despatched to Germany? After all, he was only there unofficially. It didn't seem to me that he played an active enough role in that incident for someone to want to kill him thirty years later."

"I wish I knew more about Mercer's activities in France," Bravington said. "Mercer's never talked about them, not to my knowledge anyway, and as I told you before, most of the records were destroyed."

"Could he have been used by the Gestapo for interrogating a prisoner?" Rudd asked. "Or could he have been involved in giving information that led to someone's arrest? That's the kind of question I want to find the answer to. Obviously Mercer won't tell us. If something like that did happen, he'd want to keep it quiet. Even though he was acting for the Allies, he might have been forced into betraying someone to make his cover-story seem convincing to the Germans."

"In that case, wouldn't he suspect the real identity of the person who's threatening his life?" Bravington asked. "The man's no fool."

"Possibly," agreed Rudd, "although he may, to ease his own conscience, prefer to accept the idea that it's someone connected with that train-load of prisoners. All of us are capable of self-deception if it's kinder to our esteem to fool ourselves rather than face up to an unpleasant truth."

Bravington looked at him with interest and respect.

"You have a good knowledge of human nature," he remarked.

"It's my job," Rudd replied. "Like a carpenter gets to understand wood, I get to know people. It's my stock-in-trade you might say."

He paused and then continued.

"That's why I want to go to France. I don't think we're going to achieve much if we concentrate solely on this end. We could be keeping a watch on Mercer for months."

"I see your point," Bravington replied. "I've fixed up for you to fly over to France tomorrow. The papers are all in here," he added, tapping his jacket pocket. "You won't need a passport. I've arranged identification papers that will satisfy the French authorities. I'll explain the details to you over coffee."

Rudd agreed. He had never liked talking and eating at the same time, particularly when the food was good. It spoiled his enjoyment of it. The meal continued in silence and Rudd ate his way steadily and with great satisfaction through trout cooked with almonds, steak *tartare* served with a green salad and an excellent piece of Stilton, in perfect condition.

The table was finally cleared, coffee was brought to them and, when the waiter had gone, Bravington produced a folder of papers from his inside pocket and a map from his brief-case, which he spread out for Rudd's inspection.

"There's a small private airfield here," Bravington explained, pointing to the map, "a few miles from Ipswich. I've arranged for a light plane to be ready to fly you tomorrow at 10 a.m. to another private airfield near Demour. A Monsieur Pierre Blanchard, of French Security, will be waiting there with a car. He will have driven down from Paris. He speaks excellent English, by the way, so you shouldn't have any difficulties with the language. I've spoken to him on the phone and he'll do his best to find out meanwhile what he can at his end before he meets you, although with the records largely destroyed he didn't hold out much hope. There are your identity papers," he added, passing them over to Rudd, "and some French money. It's the equivalent of about £50. If you need any more, M. Blanchard will see that you get it. I managed to get two photos of Mercer taken during the war. One is a blow-up of the original shot taken on the station, showing just his head and shoulders; the other's taken from the identity papers he had at the time. Luckily Records turned them up. They're both in this envelope. By the way, the pilot of the plane will stay at the airfield in France. There's a club-house he can put up at, so you only need to phone him to arrange your flight back."

As Rudd pocketed the papers, the French money and the photographs of Mercer, he thought that, in the short time available, Bravington had organised everything extremely well.

"If you get into any difficulties," Bravington added, "you can always phone me in London at the numbers I gave you. I've given instructions that any calls from France are to be passed to me immediately.''

He looked at Rudd and his long grey face looked longer and greyer than ever.

''You know, it's not just simply a matter of a man's life being in danger, although God knows that's serious enough. It's also a question of state security. Our agents have to be protected and I'm not at all happy that someone's found out a great deal about Mercer over the years. It may be a personal vendetta but there's more to it than just that. I want this man caught.''

''I'll do my best, sir,'' Rudd replied. He could understand Bravingon's concern. But that was his problem. Rudd's interest in the man lay only in him as a possible murderer. The question of security was something that Rudd was shrewd enough to realise he could not meddle in. Catch the man and both problems were solved. And catching him was very much his own problem.

He and Bravington parted shortly afterwards and Rudd returned to the Plough to get ready for his trip to France the following day. George and Ida shook hands with him before he left the next morning, with the hope that he'd soon get the problem of the garage settled satisfactorily and Rudd, with a wave of his hand, drove off in the direction of the main Ipswich road.

The airfield was small with a few light planes waiting on the grassed runways. It was all very casual. As Rudd parked the car and got out, a young man, cheerful, round-faced, smiling, strolled up to him, introduced himself as Ken and asked,

''You're Mr. Rudd? Flying to France?''

Rudd replied that he was and Ken replied, ''Right-oh'' and led the way towards one of the planes, remarking as he did so,

''I understand you'll give me a ring at the club about the flight back. I'll most likely be at the bar when you need me.''

Rudd climbed into the plane and strapped himself in at Ken's instructions, and a few minutes later the aircraft was airborne. It was done with as little fuss as if he was being given a lift by car to the next town.

The toy fields and houses disappeared below them and the sea, brilliant in the sunshine, its surface only faintly wrinkled with movement, took their place. They passed over a boat that seemed to lie stationary on the water, their own shadow moving swiftly across it. Shortly afterwards the low sand dunes of the French coast came into view and then they were dipping down over the countryside and taxiing along a runway of the small airfield near Demour, which, as far as Rudd could see, was almost the same as the one he had left that short time before in England.

The plane stopped, Rudd shook hands with Ken who grinned in his friendly casual way, and the Inspector clambered out and began walking towards the low, white-painted buildings on the edge of the runway. As he approached them, a tall young man who had been waiting outside came forward.

Rudd had no definite expectations of what Pierre Blanchard would look like. All the same, he was surprised to see that he was tall, thin and serious-faced, looking more like the embodiment of a typical Englishman in his formal dark suit and dazzling white shirt. He was solemn, too, and a little aloof in what is generally expected to be the English manner and, as they shook hands, Rudd wondered what Blanchard would make of him, for the Inspector had seen no need to dress up for the occasion and was wearing a pair of baggy grey trousers, a casual sports shirt and a lightweight beige jacket that had seen better days. He was carrying, too, a disreputable canvas holdall in which he had stuffed a clean shirt, a change of socks and his pyjama trousers only.

"I am delighted to meet you," Blanchard was saying. "I hope you had a good trip?"

His English was perfect; a shade too correct so that even the colloquialisms sounded like quotations from a grammar book. But then, as Rudd admitted ruefully to himself, his own French was only School Certificate standard and he had never properly mastered the use of the subjunctive.

They walked towards Blanchard's car, a well-polished Citroen that had an official look about it. Blanchard politely took Rudd's holdall and put it on the back seat alongside his own impeccable leather case and, a few minutes later, they were turning out of the airfield gates and were heading along the road that led to Demour.

Rudd was longing for a good look at the passing countryside. He knew Paris fairly well and had visited the South of France but this was the first time he had been in the *Calvados* region. But he had come here on a case and, apart from a few fleeting glimpses of fields and farms, he gave his full attention to what Blanchard was saying to him.

"Mr. Bravington telephoned me in Paris yesterday and I've done my best in the short time available to find out what I could. It's not been easy though, and I understand you have met the same difficulties yourselves. The town was heavily bombed by the Allies before it was captured and most of the records were destroyed."

The remark was made without any emotion and Rudd wondered if, for instance, London had suffered the same fate, he would be able to talk about it so calmly.

Blanchard continued.

"Most of what I have been able to discover concerns the Resistance movement in this area, although I understand Mr. Mercer was not directly concerned with them."

"I believe that's so," replied Rudd. "He did have one contact, someone unidentified through whom he passed on information. I'm afraid I don't know much about it, except that Mercer was moved out shortly after the group was rounded up by the Germans."

"They were almost certainly betrayed," Blanchard said with the same calm factual manner. "That much I have been able to discover."

Rudd tried not to show too much eagerness. Blanchard's own lack of emotion made him feel inhibited in his own reactions and, besides that, there was no evidence so far that Mercer had had any close connection with the Resistance. However, it was a possible lead that would have to be followed up. Supposing someone in that group had believed Mercer had betrayed them?

Rudd asked carefully,

"How much were you able to find out?"

"Not a lot," Blanchard admitted. "There's an official German document still in existence that refers to 'information received,' which strongly suggests betrayal, and a list of those to be brought in for questioning. It's not complete because we know more were arrested later, but it includes Marcel Gavin, the group's leader; Pierre Boileau, their radio operator; Lomel, who was an ex-convict and acted as their explosives expert, and a Monsieur Gautier who had a shipping business in Le Havre and who seemed to be concerned with smuggling people in and out of the country."

None of these names meant anything to Rudd.

"Did you come across any mention of Alec Mercer?" he asked.

"No," Blanchard replied, "but Marcel Gavin kept a sort of diary which his widow kept hidden and handed over to the authorities after the liberation. For obvious reasons, it was not a full record and many of the entries are cryptic and refer to people by initials only. There is one entry that you might find interesting, however. In October 1943, which I believe was the time Mercer arrived in France, Gavin wrote: 'New arrival. Contact made with "S." ' "

" 'S'?" asked Rudd. "Who's that?"

Blanchard shrugged.

"We don't know. It could be anybody. We're not even certain that the initials refer to real names. They may be coded."

Rudd was thinking hard.

"It's possible it refers to the contact we know Mercer had with the Resistance group."

"It's possible," Blanchard agreed but he did not sound very convinced.

"And you found out nothing more that might refer to Mercer?" Rudd persisted.

He knew before Blanchard replied that it was a fruitless question. The Frenchman lifted one hand from the steering wheel to indicate there was nothing.

"I should have thought Mercer himself would be able to supply you with more information than we can possibly find out," he commented.

"Colonel Bravington had his reasons for not questioning him," Rudd replied warily.

He was not sure how much Blanchard had been told and, anyway, there was no point in giving him too much information. He was the one who was supposed to be supplying it.

"We're approaching the outskirts of Demour now," Blanchard remarked. "Where do you want to be taken first?"

Rudd glanced out of the window. They were passing through a new housing development of modern blocks of flats that might be found anywhere in the world, except that with the beige stone trims round the windows and the shutters painted a russet brown they were unmistakably French.

"I suppose we'd better start where Mercer started: the hotel Metropole," Rudd replied.

He really had no firm ideas. The hunch that here in France where it had all happened was the place to find the answer and that yesterday had seemed so obvious, now appeared mere conjecture. There might be nothing here, after all. It had all happened so long ago and so many of those concerned with those far-off years were almost certainly dead; men like Marcel Gavin, and Lomel, who had turned from safe blowing to guerilla activities.

As if to echo Rudd's thoughts, Blanchard remarked,

"Demour is very different, of course. It's been largely rebuilt. You'll find it a very modern city, compared to what it was before the war. Only a few parts of the old town remain."

Rudd nearly sighed out loud. Documents gone. People gone.

Buildings gone. Really, if he had thought about it seriously before he set out, he might have realised that the trip was going to finish up as a wild-goose chase.

For some ridiculous reason, he began translating the phrase into French, *"Une chasse de* something-or-other *sauvage."* Except he couldn't remember the French for "goose."

"What's French for 'goose'?" he asked Blanchard.

And the Frenchman replied, without a flicker of expression, *"Oie."*

Rudd humped his shoulders despondently and slumped down in his seat. It was just his luck to get landed with someone who hadn't even a sense of humour to enliven the trip.

# 10

The hotel Metropole was near the centre of the town, facing a square with fountains and public gardens. Pierre Blanchard parked the car and Rudd, as he got out, took a quick appraising glance about him.

It was evident that all this part of the city had been rebuilt. A modern theatre with a broad flight of shallow steps and a piece of contemporary sculpture in the forecourt faced the hotel which was built in a more traditional style, in honey-coloured stone with balconies and shutters to the bedroom windows. Swing doors led them into a large pillared foyer, furnished with the international and rather anonymous luxury of any good hotel. Blanchard went over to the reception desk to consult with one of the clerks while Rudd examined some jewellery, solid chunky objects in platinum and gold, on display in one of the show cabinets.

Presently Blanchard joined him.

"Monsieur Martin, the proprietor, is busy but he will join us in the bar in a short time," he explained. "I spoke to him briefly on the house telephone and explained that we were here to make inquiries of a Paul Lamartine, which Mr. Bravington told me was the name Mr. Mercer used when he was here during the war. M. Martin remembers him and seemed only too pleased to talk about him."

"Good," replied Rudd. At least one person from those days was still alive. But when, a few minutes later, M. Martin entered the bar where they were sitting waiting for him, Rudd felt his spirits drop again. The man was only in his late forties, much too young to have been in charge of the hotel during the war.

He came forward to greet them, holding out a hand, with that well-prepared air of hospitality and smiling welcome that any good hotelier learns to cultivate. But in M. Martin's case his face robbed the expression of any bogus charm. He had one of those ugly, attractive, mobile faces that can change expression in a moment; the face of the true clown, humorous, sad, innocent and worldly-wise.

He must have caught something of Rudd's expression because, as soon as Blanchard had introduced them and they had shaken hands, he turned to the Inspector and said,

"The man who you should really be speaking to is my father. He was in charge here during the war. But he is now a very old man and has retired from business. However, I will tell you what I know about M. Lamartine. But first you must join me in a drink; an aperitif? It will soon be time for lunch."

Rudd would have preferred a beer but felt it too plebeian a drink to order in the sumptuous red-leather and polished-chromium surroundings of the bar, so he meekly ordered a Dubonnet.

When the waiter had served them, M. Martin began his story. He spoke good English, with a more obvious accent than Blanchard and with pauses from time to time while he searched for a word.

"I was about eighteen at the time that M. Paul came here to work during the war. You must forgive me if I refer to him as Paul. I did not know him by any other name. My father was in charge of the hotel then. Not this one: the original Metropole was heavily damaged and we had to have it rebuilt. Because of the war, I stayed here, working as a waiter. Normally, of course, my father would have sent me abroad, probably to England, for my training and to learn the language but during those years that was not possible.

"M. Paul came to us I believe in the autumn of 1943. Later I learnt he was working for the British. My father did not tell me this in so many words. In times of danger, it is better that even your own family do not know your secrets. Besides, the hotel was used by the German officers. There was a headquarters in the next street and they came often to the hotel to drink or to have dinner. Or to entertain their women."

He looked at Rudd, his clown's face suddenly sad.

"I know it is difficult to understand such things but many women found the German officers attractive, even those in the Gestapo. I expect it would have been the same in England if the Germans had invaded your country."

"I don't doubt it," replied Rudd.

M. Martin smiled gently, raising his shoulders and spreading out his hands in one of those Gallic gestures in which a great deal is implied.

"As I was saying, M. Paul arrived in 1943. For two or three months I did not doubt his story. It was a good one. His father, who had been an hotelier, was dead, the hotel destroyed in the British bombing. He even received letters from his mother in Rouen and had his parents' photographs in his room. He acted the part so well, including his hatred of the British for killing his father and destroying the family business. He was very friendly with the Germans, made jokes with them about the British and made much of his German grandmother. So when the German officers had a private party in the small upstairs dining-room, they always asked him to arrange it."

He smiled and nodded at Rudd.

"He was a very clever man, Monsieur, and a very brave one too, to play such a part for so long."

"How did you find out he was a British agent?" Rudd asked.

"Because of this private dining-room I told you about that the officers used. In the public rooms downstairs they had to be discreet; they couldn't drink too much in case they talked in front of the waiters. They couldn't be as free with their women because that might have led to scandal. The younger officers in particular found it troublesome. It was M. Paul who suggested they use the upstairs room. I'm afraid I can't show it to you. It no longer exists. But originally it had been designed for business conferences so it was well sound-proofed and was at a distance from the main part of the hotel. It had a small kitchen leading from it, where food sent up by lift from the kitchen downstairs could be kept hot, so there was no need for a waiter to be always present. From the German point of view it was excellent for private drinking parties where they could behave as they wished. It was also used by the more senior officers for conferences. They preferred it to their headquarters; it was more comfortable.

"It was because of this room that I discovered the truth about M. Paul. There had been some glasses smashed at a party the night before and I was sent up to check how many were broken and to replace them. The door was locked and I used my passkey to get in. When I entered, I saw M. Paul standing on the table, doing something to the chandelier that hung above it. He said first of all that it was faulty and he was trying to mend it but then he realised I had seen the length of wire that he was fastening to one of the fittings. So he laughed and said he wanted to . . ."

He broke off and turned to Blanchard.

"*Écouter aux portes*. What is that in English?"

"To eavesdrop," Blanchard replied.

"Eavesdrop?"

M. Martin seemed to be testing the flavour of the word, then raising his shoulders incredulously, he continued,

"He said the German officers told many good jokes and he wanted to listen in to them. But I was not fooled by this. I gave him a look, so."

He turned to face Rudd, lifting his eyebrows in such an exaggerated manner that they almost disappeared into his hairline.

"Then he said he would have to trust me and did I have the courage to help him, because what he had to do would be easier with two of us? I said, of course he could trust me and I would help him. He warned me that if the Germans found out what he was doing they would arrest not only him and me, but my father also, and that we would all be shot. Then he took me upstairs.

"I understood then why the week before he had asked to change his bedroom. He now had the room directly above the private dining-room. He rolled back the carpet and showed me how he had bored a hole through the floor-boards and the ceiling of the room below and fixed a wire that went down the chandelier to a small hidden microphone. In his room, the wire was to run under the boards and come up in a cupboard where he was going to place a . . ."

He flapped his hands impatiently as he sought for the right word.

". . . something so that he could listen to their conversations."

"An amplifier," suggested Rudd. "So that's how he got his information to pass on."

"And later," M. Martin continued, "he told me that he hoped to have some recording equipment sent out from England so that he could switch it on and leave it running while he was busy in another part of the hotel. He wanted me to help him push the wire under the floor-boards, which I did. I was young then and very excited at the idea that I was helping a British agent although, at the same time, I understood the danger. But later I was disappointed. I thought it would bring me closer to M. Paul, that he would treat me like a colleague; perhaps even make use of me in some important mission."

His humorous face creased up in a self-deprecatory smile.

"What really happened was that he treated me the same as usual; that is as a young boy who is not worth noticing most of the time. I understood the reason even though I was disappointed. He could not do otherwise.''

''We know he had a contact with someone in the Resistance,'' Rudd said. ''Did he ever mention this to you?''

''No. As I said, after that afternoon when I helped him with the equipment, he never again referred to his work.''

''He never mentioned anyone whose name began with 'S'?''

''No. Never.''

''Did anyone call at regular intervals at the hotel to meet him? A friend or an acquaintance?''

''No. He had free time and he usually went out alone. I don't know where he went. I must confess that at one point, soon after I discovered the truth about him, I was very curious and I thought of following him to see what he did. But I was never off duty at the same time.''

''A pity,'' said Rudd.

''Perhaps,'' conceded M. Martin. ''But I soon realised it was better that I knew as little as possible. He must have spoken to my father, warned him of what I knew, because he said to me shortly afterwards: 'Forget everything you hear or see. That way you'll live.' I saw the sense of it and I gave up the idea of trying to follow M. Paul.''

Rudd was silent for a moment. It seemed clear that whoever ''S'' was, Mercer was not in the habit of meeting him in the hotel. Perhaps they had a safer rendezvous away from the place; a small café, perhaps, or a public park.

''You were saying earlier,'' Rudd continued, ''that M. Paul was very friendly towards the Germans. Was there anyone on the staff who particularly disliked him for this reason?''

''Not that I know about,'' M. Martin replied. ''You must understand that all of us, the waiters, the barmen, the cloakroom attendants, had to pretend to be at least polite to the Germans. Some were more friendly and went out of their way to perform small services for the officers. In that way, they got bigger tips or small presents of cigarettes and soap, things that were hard to get in those days. M. Paul was not very popular because he was too friendly, especially with one officer whose name now I can't remember. I think the other members of the staff felt that M. Paul went out of his way to tell jokes against the British, for example, but we thought he did it for what he could get out of the officer. I don't think anyone looked on him as a Nazi collaborator.''

''He helped the Germans directly on one occasion,'' Rudd said.

"Did he? Then we knew nothing of that."

"So you wouldn't know if he took part, for example, in the questioning of prisoners at the German headquarters?"

M. Martin shook his head.

"No. If he did, it was kept a secret."

It was another dead end but Rudd felt he had to pursue it nevertheless.

"Were any of the staff arrested while M. Paul was working at the hotel?"

"No."

"Or any of their families or close friends?"

"Not that I know of."

"So no-one had a strong personal grudge?"

"Only one man."

Rudd sat up. Perhaps, after all, the trail was not going to peter out.

"He was a porter whose son had been a private in the French army and had been captured at the fall of France," M. Martin explained. "He hated the Germans but as he worked in the kitchen he did not come into contact with them so my father kept him on. Besides, he was a bit simple-minded."

M. Martin tapped his own forehead significantly.

Rudd slumped back. A simple-minded kitchen porter hardly fitted in with his mental picture of a man who had trailed Mercer for thirty years.

He looked at Blanchard as much as to say "I give up."

Blanchard returned the glance, his normally solemn face expressing fellow sympathy and, for the first time since they had met, Rudd felt his heart warm towards the French Security man.

"May I?" Blanchard asked politely, and when Rudd nodded his head, he took up the questioning.

"M. Paul left the hotel in the spring of 1944 I believe?"

"Yes," M. Martin replied. "A story was put about at the time that his mother was ill and he was returning to Rouen. Afterwards my father told me that many Resistance workers had been arrested and it was considered dangerous for M. Paul to stay on at the hotel. We'd heard rumours, of course, that the Germans were rounding up people."

"I understand that they were betrayed. Were there any rumours about this?"

M. Martin pulled thoughtfully at his lower lip.

"There were many stories. In war-time there are always rumours but it was not easy to find out the truth. As I understood it, they were arrested while they were trying to smuggle a British airman out of the country. One arrest led to another and soon the whole group was captured.''

Rudd broke in.

''A British airman? That's the first I've heard about him.''

''Really? I am surprised that his story is not known to you. He was a very brave man.''

''And he was captured with the others?''

''So I understand. Strangely enough, he was shot down near here in February and brought into the town for questioning at the German headquarters. Although he was wounded, he managed to escape and make his way to a café not far from here. I don't know much more about him. I don't even know where he was recaptured.''

''Did M. Paul know about him?''

M. Martin shrugged.

''I don't know. I only heard about it myself much later, after M. Paul had left the hotel.''

''You said the airman was taken to the German headquarters for questioning. Was it the same headquarters that the German officers who used the hotel were attached to?''

''I don't know. It's possible, I suppose. But every district had its own German post.''

''If it was the same,'' Rudd said, half to himself, ''I suppose Mercer could have got the story from the German officer he was friendly with.''

''It's possible,'' Blanchard agreed, ''although I don't see any real connection between Mr. Mercer and this airman.''

''Neither do I,'' replied Rudd. ''But it's the first real lead we've had and it's worth following up.''

He turned to M. Martin who had been listening to their conversation with evident interest.

''You say the British pilot went to a café? Do you know the name of it?''

''I was told once,'' he replied, ''but I have forgotten it.''

Damn! thought Rudd.

''But I can telephone to my father. He may remember it,'' M. Martin added.

''I'd be grateful if you would,'' Rudd replied.

M. Martin left the bar and returned a few minutes later, looking jaunty and pleased with himself.

"My father is very old now," he said, "but, *grâce à Dieu,* he still has a clear mind. It was a café called Au Genêt d'Or and it's in the Rue de la Chappelle, about twenty minutes walk from here. If it's still there," he added. "It may have been bombed or pulled down."

The bar was beginning to fill up and he looked at his watch.

"Is that all, gentlemen? It is nearly lunchtime and I shall have to supervise in the dining-rooms."

Rudd and Blanchard exchanged unspoken questions. They were beginning at last to establish some kind of relationship.

"I think so," Rudd replied.

"If there are any other questions you wish to ask, I am at your service, of course. And I shall be delighted if you would lunch here as my guests. I'll speak to the head-waiter. Were you thinking of staying in Demour for any length of time?"

"Possibly for a day or two," Rudd replied.

"Then I shall see that two rooms are available for you tonight in case you need them."

"You're very kind," murmured Rudd.

"Not at all," replied M. Martin. "It is a small repayment for the sort of service that men like M. Paul gave to France during the war. Now, if you will excuse me?"

He shook hands and left the bar, leaving Rudd and Blanchard to finish their drinks and afterwards to go through to the dining-room, where the head-waiter, briefed no doubt by M. Martin, served them himself and saw that they had the best of everything on the menu.

Rudd began to cheer up. Things weren't looking so bad after all. Blanchard seemed to be unbending a little and if the Inspector had learnt nothing of great value from M. Martin, at least he had a new contact to try: the café called Au Genêt d'Or, providing, of course, that it was still there.

"Did you find any reference to this British airman, whoever he was?" he asked Blanchard, as he dipped his spoon into an excellent *soupe au pistou.*

"No, not a word," Blanchard replied. "Of course, all the Resistance groups were concerned with smuggling people out of the country who were wanted by the Germans; British agents, French nationals, Allied airmen. They were usually known by code names and the group would have a whole network of contacts willing to hide someone for a few days, or weeks if necessary, before passing them on to the next."

"Where would they finish up?" Rudd asked.

"Usually at the Spanish border. There they'd be handed over to a guide who'd take them across the Pyrenees."

"I wonder . . ." Rudd began.

"What?" Blanchard asked.

"Whether Mercer played any part in it."

Blanchard looked doubtful.

"According to M. Martin, he was working here full-time with only the usual off-duty hours. It doesn't seem very likely that he'd be active in smuggling for the Resistance."

But Rudd refused to be put off. There was, he felt, some link between Mercer and the nameless British airman although what it was he had yet to find out.

There was also something else nagging away at the back of his mind; something that M. Martin had said that might be significant although he could not for the moment recall what it was. He dismissed it and turned his attention to ordering the next course. Whatever it was, he'd remember it sooner or later, if it had any real importance.

# 11

They decided to leave the car and go to the café on foot, partly to walk off the effects of the heavy lunch they had eaten; partly in order to get some idea of the town.

The afternoon was very warm and Rudd carried his jacket over his arm a little defiantly as Blanchard, unruffled and uncreased despite the heat, still retained his impeccable appearance. It had, however, ceased to bother the Inspector as much as at first. He was beginning to feel more at ease with the man and to realise that his formality might be nothing more than a protective device, behind which someone far more human and vulnerable had taken refuge.

Blanchard had obtained a street map from the reception clerk at the hotel and had marked out their route to the café. It took them through the old part of the town, untouched by the Allied bombing; an area of narrow streets and tall buildings, their stucco pock-marked and peeling. Open doorways gave glimpses of inner court-yards where washing hung from balconies and potted plants on window-sills struggled upwards towards the sun.

Rudd tried to picture the British airman walking along these streets, past the dingy bar on the corner and the local *boulangerie* with the long loaves piled up in the window, expecting any moment to hear a shout from a German soldier in a grey uniform. It had been winter then. Perhaps it was growing dark. Certainly, wounded and on the run, he must have dreaded passing every alley-way, wondered as he came to each street crossing which way to turn.

Pierre Blanchard's thoughts must have been running along the same lines because he remarked to Rudd,

"I wouldn't like to find my way through this area with the Germans out looking for me."

They had been walking for about a quarter of an hour when, turning left at the end of a narrow street, they entered the Rue de la Chappelle. Although it was still part of the old city, it was in a smarter neighbourhood, redesigned and refurbished, Rudd suspected, for the tourist trade. Small boutiques selling luxury goods, such as perfumes, furs, porcelain, took the place of the old tenement blocks. The passers-by were well-dressed and, once or twice, Rudd caught snatches of conversation in American voices.

The café Au Genêt d'Or was half-way down the street. There were no outdoor tables as the pavement was too narrow for a terrace. Rudd examined its facade briefly before they went in and guessed that it, too, must have been converted since those far-off war-time days. M. Martin had spoken of it as a "café." It was a restaurant now, fashionably provincial with red-and-white gingham curtains and a handwritten menu hanging in the window. But the Inspector hoped that, like a good many small French businesses, it had remained in the hands of the same family that had run it during the war.

The interior was larger than it appeared from the street and was empty apart from a man and woman, obviously lovers, still tête à tête at one of the tables, concentrating on each other rather than the food. A bored-looking waiter, standing against the bar at the far end, watched them with a cynical expression on his face. As Rudd and Blanchard entered, he hurried forward to serve them, pleased to welcome new customers and to have something to do other than watch the lovers holding hands and murmuring at each other.

Blanchard spoke to him quickly in French and the waiter, after giving them a look of deep suspicion, directed particularly at Rudd, went away through a curtained opening at the back of the bar.

He thinks we're from the police, Rudd thought, amused.

A few seconds later, the curtains parted again and a plump, busy-looking man in his early fifties, with a comfortable paunch that indicated many years of good living, entered. He had evidently been disturbed from his afternoon's rest as he was still adjusting his tie and the back of his hair was rumpled up. He smoothed it down quickly as he came towards them.

"Messieurs?" he inquired. His smile was affable enough but his eyes were very watchful.

Blanchard began speaking to him rapidly in French. Rudd, unable to follow the conversation except for an occasional word here and there, watched the restaurant owner's face. The expression on it changed rapidly from disguised suspicion, to surprise and then to delight and, before Blanchard had finished speaking, he turned to seize Rudd's hand and began to shake it warmly.

"Monsieur Bayard," Blanchard said, making the belated introduction.

"*Enchanté*," murmured Rudd.

Monsieur Bayard immediately broke into excited speech which Blanchard stopped with a gesture.

"He thinks you speak French," he explained to Rudd.

They were conducted with some ceremony to a corner table near the bar and the waiter, who had been watching and listening with considerable interest, was sent away to fetch drinks. He returned shortly with a bottle of cognac and some glasses and, while M. Bayard supervised the pouring of it, Blanchard said to Rudd,

"He remembers the British airman very well. I'll translate as he doesn't speak much English but you must interrupt if there are any questions you want to ask. By the way, I've said you're a writer, looking for material about famous war-time escape stories. It seemed the most discreet way to explain it."

Rudd nodded his agreement.

"He said," Blanchard continued and here he permitted himself a small smile, "that he could see you were a writer from the way you dressed."

Rudd returned the smile more broadly.

The waiter had withdrawn and M. Bayard, having taken his first appreciative sip of his brandy, began to talk. He would have gone on without pause had not Blanchard interrupted him from time to time to translate what he said for Rudd's benefit. While this was happening, the restaurant owner watched Rudd's face eagerly, anxious to know what effect his story was having on the English writer.

"He said that the British pilot came here late one afternoon in the winter of '43. He can't remember the exact date. This place was only a café then, not at all smart, used mainly by workmen. It was owned by his mother-in-law, a widow, and he and his wife, the daughter, who were newly married then, lived with her and helped to run it. It wasn't much used by the Germans although occasionally a private might come in, late at night, for a drink; so he was very surprised when a German officer entered. The man came a little way into the café and then fainted. Bayard and his wife hurried forward to help him and then discovered that, under the long grey officer's overcoat, he was wearing a British air-force uniform. Luckily the café was empty at the time. They carried him through to the room behind the bar and put him on the sofa as he was still unconscious. Old Mme. Gatin, the mother-in-law, was very worried about it. It seemed clear to them that he'd escaped and the Germans would be out looking for him. She was afraid he might be found and she wanted him taken away.

"M. Bayard didn't have any contacts himself with the Resistance but he knew of a garage proprietor in the neighbourhood who was said to go away on 'business' from time to time. In the war, this usually meant black-market dealings or work for the Maquis; something, anyway, that the Germans wouldn't have approved of. Bayard went to see him. He said he had to be very careful. He didn't want to betray the Englishman and in those days you didn't know whom you could trust. But it was all right. The garage owner told him to go home and he would send somebody to look after his 'guest.' Bayard had already told him that the airman was injured and would need a doctor. Later that evening a girl and a young man came to the café. The girl was young, very beautiful, with dark hair. He said that his wife was always careful to be present when she came, just in case her husband's attention strayed too much."

Rudd had noticed Bayard's face light up at a certain point in the preceding conversation that Blanchard was now translating and guessed it was then that the café owner was describing the girl and it struck him that the girl must have been very beautiful indeed for him to remember her with such obvious pleasure so many years afterwards.

"What did the man look like?" Rudd asked, wondering if it could have been Mercer.

Blanchard translated the questions and M. Bayard began to describe him, using his hands to sketch him in the air. But even before Blanchard could put the description into English, Rudd could tell from his gestures that it was not Mercer.

"He was short, wore glasses and had a small moustache," Blanchard said. "M. Bayard thinks he was a medical student or a young doctor just beginning to practise. He examined the pilot and said he had fractured two ribs and broken an ankle and that his right knee also was injured."

Here M. Bayard interrupted excitedly. Blanchard listened and then turned to Rudd with a smile.

"He wants you to know how brave the man was. He regained consciousness and all the time he was being examined, although it was very painful, he didn't cry out once. Ever since then, he says he has had a great admiration for the British."

Rudd smiled his pleasure and M. Bayard leaned across the table to shake his hand, pumping it up and down to show continued admiration. When this demonstration was over, Blanchard continued the story.

"The girl, who spoke English, questioned the pilot to find out what had happened. It seemed he was on a reconnaissance flight over the town when he was shot down. He parachuted out, was captured and taken to a German post for questioning. There he was put into a small room and a German officer came in for the interrogation. He was wearing an overcoat which he hung up behind the door. During the questioning, there was some kind of disturbance in the corridor outside. The airman said he could hear a woman screaming and crying hysterically. It went on for several seconds, and the officer became annoyed and left the room to find out what was happening. There was a window in the room, overlooking a courtyard, and the airman decided to try to escape. He put on the officer's greatcoat, opened the window and jumped out. It was getting dusk then. He had no idea where he was or where to go. An alley-way led out of the courtyard into a side street and he walked along, keeping as far as possible away from the busier roads. Eventually he came to this café. By that time he knew he couldn't walk any further. He was in great pain, so he came in; not caring, he said, if the Germans found him. But he was delighted that they were friendly and were going to help him escape."

Blanchard paused and M. Bayard took up the story again. At one point he pointed dramatically towards the floor.

"He says," Blanchard translated, "that the young man did what he could for the man's injuries and gave him a tablet to help kill the pain. It was clear that he could not be moved and the girl asked M. Bayard if he would be willing to hide the man until he was sufficiently recovered to be moved to another hiding-place. Bayard agreed, although his wife and mother-in-law were not very happy about it. The penalty for helping the Resistance was only too well-known. There's a cellar underneath the café and they carried him down there. The Germans would obviously make a house-to-house search in the district but he thought there was a good chance that he wouldn't be found."

M. Bayard was sketching something with his hands. A wall, was it? Or a barrier of some kind? Rudd watched the hands, fascinated.

Blanchard listened and then turned to Rudd.

"He says, if you like, he will show you where they hid him."

"Yes, I'd like to see," Rudd replied.

Even though, so far, there seemed to be no connection between the airman and Mercer, it was, nevertheless, an interesting story from the past.

They rose and followed M. Bayard behind the bar. The curtained opening gave on to a short passage. On their right was the kitchen, with a big wooden table in the centre and copper pans hanging on the wall. At the end of the passage was another door which Bayard opened, turning on an electric-light switch just inside. Stone steps led downwards and a cool, winey smell came up.

They descended the stairs into a large, clean, brick-floored cellar, its walls lined with racks of bottles. M. Bayard was indicating an area with his hands and talking volubly.

"He says the cellar was smaller then," Blanchard explained, "and had an alcove that was used for storing wood. It was just big enough to hold a bed. They put a small divan in there for the airman to sleep on and covered over the entrance with a wine rack that could be pushed out of the way when they took him food or when the doctor came to give him medical treatment. The grill in the wall is where the alcove was."

Rudd glanced up at it. It was in the back wall of the cellar and must open out into the yard behind the restaurant. Faint sunlight filtered in through the iron bars. He tried to imagine what it was like for the injured pilot, lying there, in semi-darkness, wondering if the footsteps on the stone stairs were those of a friend or an enemy.

M. Bayard shivered dramatically and pointed upwards, indicating that he thought they ought to go. It was indeed cool down there and Rudd thought how bitterly cold it must have been in that winter all those years ago.

They went up the steps, M. Bayard in front, still talking, and Blanchard passing on what he said to Rudd who came last.

"He says that, as you can see, it wasn't an ideal hiding-place, although it was safe enough. The Germans came and searched the place, including the cellar, but they didn't think to move the rack. But it was very cold down there and there was not much space to move about in. The bed took up nearly all the room. Besides, his ankle and knee weren't healing satisfactorily."

They reached the restaurant and took their seats again at the table.

"The student was worried about him. He and the girl came one evening and after they had examined him, they sat here in this very corner, discussing what to do. The student wanted him to be moved

omewhere where he could get constant medical attention. M. Bayard
ouldn't hear all that they were saying; they spoke in low voices. It
as better, anyway, in those days not to know too much. But he did
verhear the words 'Doctor Chiron' and 'St. Sauveur des Bois.' St.
auveur des Bois is a village about forty kilometres away. He
uessed they wanted to move the airman there where the local doctor
vould be willing to look after him.

"Two days later they came back and asked him to leave the
ate to the yard and the back door unbolted that night. About four
'clock in the morning he heard someone moving about downstairs
ut he didn't get up. He realised they were taking the British pilot
way. A little while later he heard a cart move off down the street
nat runs behind the restaurant. He remembered then that it was market
ay in the town, when the farmers used to bring in produce from
ne country to sell; so that's probably how they smuggled him out,
idden in one of the farmers' carts. Weeks later he heard the
Resistance group had been broken up. The garage proprietor and his
vife were arrested. He was worried about the young girl and the
tudent and also about the airman but he couldn't find out anything.
t wasn't wise to ask too many questions but a neighbour told him
bout the garage owner and his wife. The Gestapo came for them
ne morning and they've never been seen since. A grandmother later
ook their two children, a boy and a girl, back with her to her home.
He thinks to Bordeaux but he's not sure. There was a rumour about
doctor in one of the villages being sent to a concentration camp
nd he wondered if it was the same doctor he'd heard the girl
nention. As for the British airman, he doesn't know what happened
o him."

As Blanchard finished speaking, M. Bayard leaned forward and
addressed Rudd directly, his plump face very solemn and earnest.

"He says if you could find out, he and his wife would be very
grateful. If he's still alive, perhaps you would give him their good
wishes and tell him that if he is ever in Demour he mustn't forget to
come and see them. His wife is out at the moment; it's their quietest
ime and she's gone to the hairdresser's but he knows that she'll join
aim in sending the British airman their very best wishes."

"Of course," Rudd replied, touched by the man's obvious
sincerity and concern over the fate of that unknown Englishman who
nad entered their lives all those years ago.

They shook hands and left, M. Bayard escorting them to the
door, exhorting them both to come and dine with him if they were

ever in the town again and wishing Rudd every success with his book
which the Inspector thanked him for gravely.

"Was that any help?" asked Blanchard as they walked away.

"I don't know," Rudd confessed. "On the face of it, it has no
obvious connection with Mercer, except the rather weak link he had
with the Resistance group through the contact known as 'S.' Yet I
can't see any other lead developing. We've drawn a blank at the
hotel. No-one working there seemed to have a grudge against Mercer
so we're left with the Resistance group. There's evidence that they
were betrayed. Supposing someone believes it was Mercer who
betrayed them? After all, he was playing a double game, pretending
to be friendly with the Germans. We know it was a bluff. But
supposing someone really thought he was acting as an undercover
agent? Infiltrating himself into the Resistance group and then giving
them away?"

Blanchard looked animated for the first time since Rudd had
met him.

"It makes sense!" he cried. "All we need to do is to check up
on the families of those we know were in the group . . ."

"Which will take time," Rudd pointed out.

"Of course," Blanchard agreed. "It will mean making a thorough search of any records still in existence, tracing back the
names . . ."

His brief animation died away. Rudd gave him a sour grin.

"And as most of the group are dead, it's not going to be easy.
According to M. Bayard, at least five people were rounded up that
he knows about: the garage owner and his wife, the girl, the student
and the doctor."

"And the others, too, that I mentioned," Blanchard added.
"Marcel Gavin, Pierre Boileau, Lomel and M. Gautier; and presumably Mercer's contact, 'S.' At least, he was not active when the
group was re-formed later with new people."

"Any leads on them?" Rudd asked.

Blanchard shrugged.

"It's possible. We know Mme. Gavin was alive in '45, when
she handed over her husband's diaries. Whether she is still alive or
not, I don't know. As for the others, we could make inquiries."

"Well, the people Bayard mentioned are a wash-out to start
with," Rudd replied. "The girl and the medical student were unknown to him. He didn't even know their names. The garage owner
and his wife never returned and are presumably dead; the children

ere taken away by their grandmother, possibly to Bordeaux, but
e don't even know that for certain. Which leaves the doctor.''

"At least we know where he lived," Blanchard said.

"Exactly," Rudd agreed. "If he's still alive, which I very
much doubt, we may be able to pick up some information. It's a
ong shot, but at least it's something definite to go on.''

Blanchard glanced at his watch.

"We could drive over there now," he said. "If it's only forty
kilometres away, it should take less than an hour.''

Rudd humped his shoulders. The optimism he had felt at
lunchtime had already faded, leaving him tired and dispirited. Would
that trip turn out to be yet another *"chasse d'oie sauvage"*? Even if
it was, he supposed he was obliged to follow it up, although so far
he seemed to have learnt nothing that was of any real significance to
the case.

It was not the journey that had exhausted him. Under normal
circumstances he would have welcomed it as a break from routine. It
was more a psychological weariness that had been developing ever
since he took on the Mercer case: a sense of frustration; of getting
nowhere. He had been so sure that, once in France, things would be
different. But the old pattern was repeating itself, as if circumstances
had lined themselves up against him.

Blanchard gave him a quick look, full of genuine understanding.

"No, we'll go tomorrow," he said decisively. "You look tired
and, besides, it may take some time finding the right people to talk
to. Instead we'll take a stroll through the city. You can't come to
Demour and see nothing except one hotel and one restaurant.''

It said much for Rudd's low state of mind that he welcomed the
decision being made for him.

They walked slowly, making for the heart of the town where
the river ran between tree-lined *quais* and a huge, paved market-
square was situated just off the main bridge. The market was still in
progress, the stalls covered with striped awnings, although, here and
there, a peasant farmer or his wife, unable perhaps to afford a stall,
stood at the pavement's edge with a basket of eggs for sale, or
home-made cheese or a couple of live hens, their feet tied together.

Blanchard and Rudd propped themselves against the coping of
the *quai* wall, the bustle and activity of the market behind them, in
front of them the swiftly moving water and in the distance the cranes
that marked the port, lifting up against the late afternoon sky. A boat
was being unloaded. Great bulks of timber swung across space and

then disappeared behind the warehouses. To their right, the twi
Gothic towers of the cathedral, untouched by the war, rose above th
houses and blocks of flats.

It had all changed, of course. Except for the huddled roofs o
the old town, every other building was modern. If Mercer returned
he probably wouldn't recognise it. The river, of course, was th
same and Rudd wondered if he and ''S'' had ever met in the ver
spot where he and Blanchard were standing now, leaned like then
on the wall and watched the water flow past below them.

Suddenly Rudd became alert. A new idea, so simple, so obvi
ous, that he couldn't think why he had not thought of it before
occurred to him. He was looking for someone who knew Merce
well, who had had close contact with him and who believed tha
Mercer had betrayed him. Who better fitted that bill than ''S'
himself? After all, he was Mercer's only contact with the Resis
tance. Suppose, when they were rounded up, ''S'' believed it wa
Mercer who had given them away? Suppose ''S'' was still alive'
There was no evidence that he had been captured. Blanchard hac
merely surmised that he had, because he was not active again wher
the group re-formed. But that was only negative evidence. It provec
nothing. The man might have escaped capture and rejoined the
group under another name.

He half turned to Blanchard, eager to communicate this new
idea, and then stopped himself from doing so.

There would be time enough tomorrow, after they had followec
up the lead in St. Sauveur des Bois. After all, there might be
someone there, the doctor himself if he was still alive, who could
put a definite identification to the mysterious ''S.''

It was about time that something positive turned up, Rudd
reckoned, and he felt his former optimism return.

# 12

They spent the night at the hotel Metropole in considerable comfort and the next morning, after breakfast, set out for the village of St. Sauveur des Bois.

Blanchard drove fast but with an air of easy competence. He kept his attention on the road and Rudd, busy with his own thoughts, was glad of the silence. The *Calvados* countryside flashed past the windows, very English in many ways with fields of corn and crops and clumps of trees surrounding old farmhouses, some of them beamed and plastered. And yet it was foreign at the same time. The trees were different in shape for one thing; taller and thinner than their English counterparts and most of the farmhouses had great wood-piles against their walls and orchards of gnarled apple trees from whose fruit the famous cider of the district was produced.

St. Sauveur des Bois was more of a small town than a village, with a straight road running through it, lined with pollarded plane trees. Blanchard asked directions of a passer-by and was directed to the town square which lay just off the main street with the *Mairie* on one side, flying the tricolour; the school, a grim building behind high spiked railings, was on another side with the huge bulk of the church of St. Sauveur facing it. The remaining side of the square contained private houses, solid and built of stone and, from their air of respectability, Rudd guessed they were the homes of the local dignitaries. Blanchard pointed out one as being the doctor's house.

Rudd elected to stay in the car while Blanchard made inquiries. A young woman answered the door to him, much too young to have any connection with the people concerned in the case; she could not

have been more than a baby when Mercer and "S" and the British
airman were engaged in their war-time activities.

Presently Blanchard returned and spoke to Rudd through the
open window of the car.

"She's heard of Dr. Chiron. It seems he's quite a hero in the
town; people still speak of him, at least the older ones who were
alive during the war. He died in a concentration camp."

Rudd pulled a wry face. It seemed once more they were going
to draw a blank. Seeing his expression, Blanchard smiled, his
solemn face lighting up.

"I know how you feel," he said, "but it's not all bad news.
There's an old priest, retired now, who may be able to help us. He
was evidently very friendly with the doctor and may know some
details about him. He lives in a house behind the church. I think he's
worth talking to, don't you?"

Rudd agreed and the two men set out on foot for the church that
lay across on the other side of the square. A narrow street of small
houses ran down the side of it, the doors set open in the warmth of
the morning. Geraniums stood on windowsills and a bird sang
sweetly in its cage hung outside on a wall. At the end of the street a
lane-led off to the left, passing between the high stone facade of the
church on one side and a garden wall, in which house leeks and red
valerian had taken root in the old brickwork, on the other. It was hot
in the narrow enclosed space and Rudd longed to take off his jacket
but he was not sure that he ought to. A visit to an old retired French
priest called perhaps for more formal wear than shirt-sleeves.

Half-way down the lane they came to a wooden door, painted
green, set into the brick wall, and beside it hung an old-fashioned
brass bell-pull, shaped like a stirrup, attached to a chain that disappeared into a hole in the jamb.

Blanchard gave it a pull and they heard faintly from inside a
bell ringing unevenly. For a few moments nothing happened and
Blanchard was about to give it another tug, when there was a rattle
behind the door of bolts being drawn and it was opened by a gaunt,
thin-faced woman dressed entirely in black, her grey hair drawn
back into a severe bun, and wearing round her neck a heavy silver
crucifix on a chain that seemed to Rudd to be more penitential than
ornamental.

She looked at them both suspiciously and said something in
French which Rudd guessed from her expression was the equivalent
of "Well, what do you want?"

Blanchard spoke to her politely and she seemed to soften a little but not enough to allow them inside. The door was closed in their faces and Blanchard turned to Rudd with an amused and apologetic air.

"She's gone to ask Father Tabard's permission," he explained. "She says he's a very old man and doesn't often receive visitors."

"She's his housekeeper?" Rudd hazarded.

"Undoubtedly," Blanchard replied. "And typical of many women who give up their lives to the Church. Not quite devout enough to be nuns, you can see them any day in almost any church in France; on their knees, praying; or cleaning the floors. Perhaps they hoped once for marriage but, as they get older, they light candles to the saints."

At this point the door was re-opened and the housekeeper motioned them inside with a movement of her head. As soon as they entered, she closed and bolted the door behind them.

They found themselves in a walled courtyard garden, paved with bricks and so bursting with plants and trees that it was like being in a miniature jungle. Ahead of them through the branches of some pleached apple trees that lined the path, Rudd glimpsed the upper storey of a house with grey-painted shutters and a little balcony with an ornamental iron railing. It was covered with climbing roses and vines and seemed, too, to be engulfed in leaves.

They followed the black figure of the housekeeper down the path which opened out into a paved patio, sheltered from the sun by a rose arbour. In its shade, in a wicker bath-chair, sat a very old bent man who, despite the heat, had a bright blue blanket tucked over his legs and knees.

Apart from a few fine wisps of white hair, his head was completely bald and Rudd noticed the brown patches on the scalp, known sometimes as gravemarks, and the same blotches on his fragile hands that lay, trembling, on the rug. But his eyes were still intelligent and bright and as Blanchard introduced him, Rudd noticed that the priest searched his face with interest and humour.

"Ah, an Englishman," he said, in English, and nodded his head several times as if this information gave him a certain personal satisfaction and even a little amusement.

The housekeeper had brought two upright dining-room chairs from the house and placed them formally side by side facing the old man, like an interview at school.

"Please to sit down," Father Tabard said.

His English was good but with a strong accent.

They sat, Rudd surreptitiously shifting his chair a little out of line. This did not go unnoticed by the old man, who watched, smiled and then said something to Blanchard in French.

"Father Tabard says that he understands English better than he can speak it; so, if you would like to ask him questions in English, he will do his best to reply, but he may need to have some of his answers translated."

Rudd nodded. He was already beginning to feel at a disadvantage. The heat striking back from the paving-stones, the great age of Father Tabard, the formal arrangement of the chairs, even the chairs themselves that, with their slippery leather seats and high, carved backs, were almost impossible to relax in, made him feel uncomfortable and ill at ease.

His usual interviewing technique, the relaxed pose, the listening attitude, the gossipy approach, that encouraged the person he was questioning to talk naturally, was out of the question. He was not even sure that the old man would understand all that he said and certainly there would be no opportunity for any jocular remark to ease the tension.

The old priest was waiting for him to begin, looking at him from under shaggy white eyebrows. Rudd leaned forward.

"Monsieur," he said, "you may be able to help save the life of an Englishman."

He had hoped this dramatic opening would have some effect but he was mistaken. The priest's eyes did not blink or waver. They went on steadily regarding the Inspector and all he said in reply was,

"I understand."

For a moment Rudd was taken back by this apparent lack of response and then he suddenly realised that this old man had seen as much, if not more, of human nature than the Inspector himself. He had, after all, lived through the Nazi occupation. He must have been present at many death-beds and listened to countless confessions. Life had ceased to surprise him but, in old age, he had reached the point of understanding and accepting it.

Rudd shifted in his chair and began again.

"I believe you knew Dr. Chiron who used to practise in this town?"

"I did," replied Father Tabard. "He was a good friend. We used to drink a glass of wine together often in the evenings."

"Did you know he worked for the Resistance during the war?"

The priest lifted his hands in a gesture of impatience.

"Of course. But you mentioned an Englishman. What has he to do with the doctor?"

"Perhaps a great deal," replied Rudd. "I think something happened in the winter of 1943 that may still be affecting other people's lives."

He paused and then added gently, "A betrayal."

The old priest closed his eyes and leaned back in his chair.

"An English pilot?" Rudd prompted quietly, assuming the old man was making an effort to remember.

Father Tabard opened his eyes and looked at Rudd.

"I know what you are speaking of," he replied. "I am trying to think why this should put an Englishman in danger. As far as I know, only French people suffered. Or do you mean the pilot who was hidden by the doctor?"

"No," replied Rudd. "Another Englishman."

"Then I don't understand," the priest replied, raising his shoulders. "But I'll tell you what I know; not everything because some of the story, as you will see, I am not free to tell."

Rudd, trying not to show his disappointment, composed his face into an expression of gratified interest.

"Henri Chiron had been a doctor in this town for nearly thirty years. When the war came, he was in his fifties, a widower, with a housekeeper, a woman in her thirties to look after him. He was a good patriot and hated to see the Germans occupy his country but what could he do? He was too old to fight with the Maquis. Besides, the people in the town needed him as a doctor. But he did what he could. He offered his house and his services to the Resistance. If one of them was wounded, he would treat him. If a Maquis member needed food and shelter, he would hide him. His house was one of the 'stations' as they were called, on the route used to smuggle out Frenchmen in danger or Allied airmen who had been shot down into Free France or Spain. There was a big attic in his house. Part of it was boarded up and a small secret room made where a man could hide for weeks if necessary before being passed on to the next 'station.'

"The English pilot was brought to him in February of 1944. He had been hidden in Demour but he was injured and needed medical help. Eventually, when he had recovered, he was moved on to the next station, a farmhouse near the village of Ternes. A little while later, the doctor and the housekeeper were arrested after the Germans had been to the farm where the pilot was discovered in one of the barns. The farmer, a man called Huchette, heard them coming and shot first his wife, then his two children and then himself. He knew what would happen to them if the Germans arrested them. The doctor died a year later in a concentration camp. The housekeeper was held for questioning but was allowed later to go free as she appeared to know nothing of the doctor's connections with the Maquis.''

"And the pilot?" Rudd asked.

The priest shrugged.

"I don't know. He was taken, I believe, to a prisoner-of-war camp. He may still be alive. The Germans obeyed certain rules of war, you understand. They did not usually torture or starve Allied prisoners; only the members of the Maquis, good Frenchmen and women who were fighting to save their country.''

It was not said with any bitterness but in a calm and matter-of-fact manner, and yet Rudd felt uncomfortable. As an Englishman, what knowledge did he have of the horrors of enemy occupation?

"I believe others were arrested as well?" he said.

"Yes. Some I know only by name. Dr. Chiron knew he could trust me and I was asked sometimes to go to his house to serve mass or hear confession from a Maquis member who was hiding there. Pierre I know was shot. He was the son of the schoolmaster at Ternes. And Jules, too, whom I never met, but I often heard the doctor speak of him. Jeannette, a young nurse who fought with the Maquis, also died and a man they called Little Louis. And Simone, too, of course.''

"Simone?" asked Rudd.

"It was she who brought the men to the doctor's house to be hidden.''

"A young girl was she?" Rudd asked, remembering what Bayard had told him. "Dark-haired? Pretty?"

"Ah yes," replied Father Tabard. "Young and beautiful and very brave.''

He closed his eyes again for a moment as if recalling her to memory. "The Germans came for her in her *apartment* in Demour. The building is no longer there, I understand. It was bombed later in the war. She saw their cars in the street below and she knew there was no escape so she jumped from the window. It was on the third storey. But, *hélas,* she did not die. Although she was badly injured that did not stop them from questioning her. She died several days later as a result of it.''

Rudd bit his thumb-nail and glanced at Blanchard who was sitting in silence beside him, listening to the old man's words. The

Inspector would have liked to get up quietly, to apologise and take his leave. He felt he was reviving old painful memories that were better left undisturbed. And yet he knew he could not let the story remain incomplete. He was no nearer the truth than he had been in the restaurant Au Genêt d'Or. All he had learned were more details of the background and of the events but nothing of the actual betrayal.

He took out his wallet and handed Father Tabard the photograph of Mercer taken at the station in Demour.

"Who betrayed them?" he asked. "Was it this man?"

The old priest studied the photograph for a few seconds and then handed it back to Rudd.

"No," he said. "It was not him."

His eyes, old and faded but as clear and as candid as a child's, gazed steadily into Rudd's. The Inspector believed him.

"But you know who betrayed them?" he said. It was a shot in the dark and yet, as he said it, Rudd was convinced that the old man knew the secret.

Father Tabard nodded his head slowly, keeping his eyes on Rudd. Blanchard recrossed his legs sharply, betraying his excitement.

"Who was it?" persisted Rudd.

"Monsieur," Father Tabard said courteously and firmly, "I cannot tell you. I would be breaking the seal of silence of the confessional. All I can say is this: whoever betrayed them has paid for that betrayal in many years of suffering and contrition, but has, at last, found peace with God. Not even you can ask for that peace to be destroyed."

"But a man's life may be in danger!" Rudd cried.

He felt angry and baffled. It was as if a door had partly opened, giving him a glimpse of knowledge at last, and then, at the last moment, it was slammed shut in his face.

Father Tabard remained unmoved by his angry protest.

"Let me ask you a question," he said. "For what reasons would someone seek to take another person's life?"

Rudd frowned impatiently. If the old man was not going to come out with the truth, then Rudd was in no mood to play riddles.

"Fear? Hatred?" he suggested sharply.

Father Tabard smiled and turned to Blanchard.

"And you? What do you think?"

Blanchard raised his shoulders.

"Jealousy?" he suggested.

The priest turned back to Rudd.

"It is easy to see you are an Englishman," he said, still smiling gently. "Monsieur Blanchard is French and he understands these things much better."

It was an enigmatic remark and Rudd had the feeling that it was meant to convey some special meaning but one which he could not for the moment puzzle out.

"The French law, I understand, is different to the English," Father Tabard continued in a factual manner, as if beginning on an entirely new subject. "In France we recognise the *crime passionnel:* the crime committed out of passion. We have a certain sympathy for the husband who shoots his wife's lover out of jealousy, or the girl who kills the man who has betrayed her love. In your country, I believe, this is not so. It's the result, no doubt, of your Anglo-Saxon temperament and the nonconformist Church."

This wry comment was made with a sweet smile and a mischievous twinkle in his eyes.

"I can tell you no more, monsieur," he said. "If there are any questions you wish to ask me, I shall try to answer them."

"Only one," said Rudd. "Did you ever hear of anyone known as 'S'?"

"No," replied Father Tabard. "I have told you all the names of those I knew were connected with the Maquis group. With one exception."

"The name of the person who betrayed them?" hazarded Rudd.

The old priest bowed his head in what Rudd took to be agreement but he said nothing.

So that nice little theory was a dead loss, too, Rudd thought. If Mercer had not betrayed them and Father Tabard, who seemed to know the truth, had not heard of "S," it hardly seemed likely that the man known as "S" was the person who was now seeking Mercer's life.

"There are no more questions," Rudd said, trying to hide his bitter disappointment.

"Then my housekeeper, Mlle. Giraud, will show you out," the old priest replied, ringing a little brass bell that hung at the side of the bath-chair.

Rudd rose and took one of the frail hands.

"Thank you," he said. "I hope I have not tired you."

"I am an old man," Father Tabard replied. "I am used to being tired."

The housekeeper had emerged from the house and came to

stand behind the old man's chair. With her grim face and black clothes she put Rudd in mind of a female jailer.

Blanchard also took his leave, murmuring something in French, and the two men followed the woman down the path to the door in the garden wall. Mlle. Giraud spoke to neither of them and silently drew the bolts to let them out. Before stepping out into the lane, Rudd turned his head for a final backward glance. Nothing was visible of Father Tabard through the leaves, except for a patch of blue that was probably the blanket he wore over his knees.

It had been, Rudd thought, an unsatisfactory interview. Much had been said and yet there was still much more that lay unspoken beneath the surface; not only the identity of the person who had betrayed the Resistance group.

The Inspector was no further forward in discovering what part, if any, Mercer had played in that tragedy so many years before. Men and women had died. Their names lingered in his mind. Pierre, Jules, Jeannette, Simone, Louis. And others, too, that Blanchard had mentioned and probably more still that no-one knew about.

Their deaths and Mercer's life. He could not see that there was any possible connection. And yet he felt instinctively that he had been nearer the truth in that old man's garden than at any other time during the whole investigation.

They began to walk up the lane. Behind them Mlle. Giraud closed and fastened the door with a great rattle of bolts that had a finality in the sound. Whatever the truth was, it did not seem to the Inspector that he was ever likely now to discover it.

# 13

They walked back towards the centre of the town in silence. The heat was now intense and Rudd, disregarding propriety, took off his jacket and tie and went shirt-sleeved and open-necked. Blanchard, who did not seem to feel the heat and looked as impeccable as ever, looked slightly amused as Rudd rolled up his sleeves and stuffed his tie into his trouser pocket.

Perhaps he thought of it as just another example of English eccentricity.

"A drink?" he suggested as they approached a café. It was on the shady side of the street with a small terrace enclosed with shrubs in white-painted boxes. Wicker chairs and glass-topped tables stood invitingly under a striped awning.

"A beer," said Rudd sitting down.

The waiter came out to serve them and Blanchard ordered the beer and a Pernod for himself, and then turned to the Inspector.

"Was that a useful meeting?" he asked.

"Not really," Rudd confessed.

He was feeling very tired now; not just physically exhausted but psychologically worn out. He had run out of ideas. More than that, he had run out of hope. When it came to assessing the facts, he knew little more of real value than he had learned at that first meeting with Bravington. There had been a betrayal. Mercer's life was in danger.

The beer, when it came, was cool but thin and flat. As he drank it, Rudd suddenly wished for a pint of bitter, drunk standing at the bar of the Plough, while he listened to George gossiping easily in his soft Suffolk voice and Mercer a million miles away.

Blanchard poured a little water into his Pernod and Rudd watched it cloud and turn milky.

"I felt he was trying to tell us something," he remarked.

"Who?" growled Rudd.

"Father Tabard."

"Nothing much that was of any use to me," Rudd replied grumpily.

Blanchard was silent for a moment, tapping his fingers gently on the glass top of the table.

"I think," he said, "he was trying to suggest a motive for the betrayal."

Rudd sat up with renewed interest.

"Jealousy?" he said. He could not resist adding, "As an Anglo-Saxon and a nonconformist, I'm not supposed to know anything about that."

Blanchard laughed.

"I think Father Tabard was having a little fun at your expense. Like many Frenchmen, he has a love-hate relationship with the English. All the same, I think there was some truth in what he said. Consider some of your great classic English murders. What have been the motives behind them? Fear, as you suggested. Or greed. Or hatred. But, as he said, you do not recognise the murder that is committed for love."

"For love?" said Rudd, unable to keep the scorn out of his voice.

"You see, you don't accept it," Blanchard pointed out. "You say 'love' as if it is something you don't quite believe in. But imagine someone who could kill for love so profound, so passionate, that it turns to terrible jealousy. I'm not suggesting that you English are not capable of feeling jealousy. Of course you are. There have been murders for this motive in England too. But, in France, as Father Tabard pointed out, it would be a mitigating circumstance. In England this is not so. The last woman to be hanged in your country, if you remember, was found guilty of shooting her lover. That did not save her from the gallows. In France, the court would have recognised that she was suffering from such emotions that she could not control her actions. I think the priest was trying to tell us that the person who betrayed the others did so out of jealousy."

Rudd took another gulp of beer as he considered this.

"A man jealous of a woman?" he suggested.

"Or a woman of a man," Blanchard pointed out.

"But who?" Rudd asked. "And where does Mercer fit into

this? Father Tabard didn't recognise his photograph and yet he admits he knows the identity of the person who betrayed them. So it can't be Mercer. And if it wasn't Mercer, why should someone be trying to kill him now out of revenge?''

"I don't know," Blanchard admitted.

"Neither do I. It doesn't make any sense," Rudd replied.

He was beginning to feel disgruntled. The trip had been a complete waste of time as far as he could see. He would have been better employed concentrating on the English side of the investigation. And yet he had been so sure that the secret lay in France. He was bitterly and almost childishly disappointed, like a small boy who has been promised a treat and then had it refused.

"Don't look round," Blanchard was saying quietly, "but Father Tabard's housekeeper is on the other side of the road. She's seen us and I have the feeling she wants to talk to us."

Rudd lit a cigarette, moving his chair slightly as if searching in his pocket for his matches. The new angle allowed him an oblique view of the opposite pavement. Mlle. Giraud, wearing a black hat and carrying a basket on one arm, was standing in front of the baker's shop looking into the window as if examining the loaves. But from the furtive glances she kept making over her shoulder at the two men seated at the café table, it was not the bread on display that she was interested in.

She walked on a few paces, glanced across at them again, hesitated at the edge of the road as if she intended crossing and then, changing her mind turned back.

"Keep talking," said Rudd. "Don't let her know we've seen her."

He had a better view of her now that she had moved up the street. She stopped again, this time outside a hardware shop, and was bending down as if to examine the price tickets on a pile of cheap earthenware pots that were stacked up on a trestle table in front of the window. But she was a bad actress. She still could not resist taking little backward glances at the two men.

Rudd cheered up. The sight of that angular black-dressed figure, so obviously longing to cross the road and speak to them and yet hesitating to do so amused him. He winked at Blanchard and Blanchard surprisingly winked back, dropping one eyelid in an over-emphasised manner that gave his long serious face for a second a comic, lop-sided look.

"She'll come," said Rudd, puffing comfortably at his cigarette.

"You think so?" asked Blanchard.

"Of course," said Rudd. "Her curiosity's roused. Once you get a woman curious, there's no stopping her."

One up for the English, he thought. We may not know much about passion, but there's still a thing or two we don't need to be told about women.

He was right. Mlle. Giraud turned away from her inspection of the pots, looked directly at them and then, grasping her basket firmly in one hand, came marching across the street towards them. She had made up her mind.

"What did I tell you?" said Rudd.

Even so, at the last moment she nearly lost her nerve. As she drew level with them she hesitated and then, averting her head, began walking rapidly past them.

Rudd jumped to his feet.

"Mademoiselle Giraud!" he called after her.

She turned and slowly came back.

"Won't you sit down?" Rudd asked.

He doubted if she understood the words but the action of pulling out one of the wicker chairs at their table and gesturing towards it was obvious. She sat down reluctantly, smoothing down the dull black fabric of her dress over her knees.

"A coffee?" Rudd asked.

She looked dumbly at Blanchard who repeated the words in French, then she shook her head.

Rudd crushed out his cigarette in the white china ash-tray on the table that advertised a well-known aperitif in black lettering round the rim. For the first time since his arrival in France, he felt really frustrated by the barrier of language. If only she had been English, he would have known exactly how to deal with her. He would have put on his avuncular expression, kindly and sympathetic, with a bit of a twinkle to acknowledge her femininity, thus flattering and soothing her into talking.

She was looking at him, her gaunt face even more fleshless under the shadow of the awning. As a young woman her eyes must have been her best feature, dark, deep-set, heavy-lidded. Now they were too hollow and the expression in them was brooding and intense, like some great tragic bird.

Rudd thought he also detected a flash of fear.

Blanchard was talking to her quietly in French and she gave her attention to him, listening and looking down into her lap, her hands restlessly smoothing her dress.

Rudd tried to follow the conversation, straining every listening nerve in order to pick out any recognisable word that might give him a clue. But it was from their expressions and the movements of their hands that he learned most.

The housekeeper seemed worried by Rudd's presence. She looked at him directly, raising one hand from her lap to indicate him. Blanchard appeared to be soothing her. Several times Rudd caught the words "*anglais*" and "*la guerre*."

After a few moments, Blanchard translated.

"Mlle. Giraud wants to know why you have come to France. She asked if the family of the English airman sent you?"

Rudd was surprised at this. What business was it of hers, he asked himself, and why should she be enough concerned about it to follow them in order to ask?

"I told her," Blanchard went on, "that this wasn't the reason why you'd come to St. Sauveur. She then said that she understood the English pilot was still alive, that the Germans took him to a prisoner-of-war camp and she assumes that, after the war, he was released."

"I expect so," replied Rudd, still puzzled. "Tell her Father Tabard gave me that information."

As Blanchard translated, instead of being reassured she became more agitated, interrupting him to speak rapidly, her hand now alive with movement, making small desperate gestures. At the end, she began to cry, one limp hand resting, as if in supplication, on Blanchard's arm.

It was a pitiful and embarrassing spectacle. Rudd, who hated to see any woman cry, especially a plain and elderly spinster, looked rapidly about him. Luckily the terrace was empty apart from the three of them and there were no passers-by to witness the scene. But the waiter, drawn no doubt by the sound of her voice, was peering at them through the glass panel of the door. Rudd waved him angrily away.

Blanchard, as embarrassed as the Inspector, was patting the woman's hand with nervous rapidity.

Rudd asked quietly, "What did she say?"

Blanchard shrugged and raised his eyebrows, indicating that even he was not sure what it was all about.

"She seems worried about Father Tabard," he replied. "She says he's an old man now and sometimes forgets things. She kept repeating it was all a long time ago and there's been a lot of suffering. At the end, she just cried out 'Oh God, I wish I was dead, too, like the others!' "

Rudd looked down at her bent head, at the tight little bun of grey hair sticking out under her ugly black hat, at the scrawny neck and the heavy silver chain round it like a penance.

And suddenly he understood.

"Mademoiselle," he said softly, "you were Dr. Chiron's housekeeper?"

Blanchard, after a brief surprised glance at the Inspector, repeated the words in French, almost exactly echoing the gentle inflection in Rudd's voice.

Her bent head nodded and she scuffled in her worn leather handbag for a handkerchief.

There were other questions he could have asked her but it would have been too cruel. Instead, he produced the photograph of Alec Mercer and, touching her on the arm, showed it to her.

"Ask her if she knows this man," he said to Blanchard.

She kept the handkerchief to her mouth and above it her eyes, blurred with tears, were bewildered. She shook her head.

Rudd returned the photograph to his wallet and signalled to the waiter who, by reason of his white apron, could be seen still hovering inside the café within sight of the door.

"Un cognac," Rudd ordered when he came.

She drank it reluctantly, like medicine, but it seemed to have some effect. She was calmer afterwards, with the exhausted listlessness of someone after an emotional storm.

"Take her back to the house," Rudd said to Blanchard. "I don't think she ought to go alone."

This was largely his motive but he also wanted to be alone himself, to think. More pieces had been added to the puzzle and one mystery at least had been solved, but as yet he could not see how it affected Alec Mercer.

Blanchard murmured something to her and she nodded and got to her feet. Rudd watched them walk up the street together; the tall, thin figure of the Frenchman bending solicitously down towards the small French spinster, who seemed to have aged ten years during that interview and who now walked with the stooped shoulders and shuffling uncertain gait of a very old woman.

Rudd thought of her returning to that house, to old Father Tabard sitting in the sunlit courtyard under the rose arbour, to their shared memories and secrets.

Life went on, though, even for them. After all, she had survived for thirty years with her intolerable burden of guilt and he, the old priest, had kept the secret and remembered the dead.

Rudd ordered another beer and was half-way through it when Blanchard came walking briskly back.

"I left her at the gate," he said. "She wouldn't let me go inside with her."

"Better that way," murmured Rudd.

At least, alone, she would be able to face Father Tabard for only he knew her secret, understood and forgave her.

Blanchard said, "That was clever of you, to realise she was Dr. Chiron's housekeeper."

"It seemed the only explanation," Rudd replied. "Father Tabard hinted at the truth but left it to our knowledge of human nature to puzzle it out for ourselves. The facts were there, if we cared to take notice of them. Do you remember what he said? That the doctor was a widower; that he had a housekeeper in her thirties; that Simone, who was young and pretty, often came to the house; that the motive was jealousy. I didn't see it then but I do now. Mlle. Giraud must have loved Dr. Chiron for years, hoping that one day he might notice her as a woman and ask her to marry him. Then this young girl started coming to the house. There must have been whispered conversations, mysterious telephone calls, letters coming to the house with a Demour postmark. She must have jumped to the conclusion that the doctor was having an affair with the girl. She probably didn't realise the secret work they were both doing for the Maquis until later, after the first seeds of jealousy had been sown, and then it was too late. It didn't matter that Simone was working for the Resistance, that she brought people to be hidden from the Germans and arranged for them to be moved on to the next hiding-place. But this knowledge gave Mlle. Giraud a terrible power over Simone and the doctor. I wonder what finally decided her to use it? Perhaps the doctor spoke angrily to her one day. Perhaps she felt the girl slighted her. We'll never know. But we've seen enough this morning to know that she's an emotional and impulsive woman who acts without thinking. She followed us today because she had to find out why we were here. I think she was worried because I was English and was making inquiries about the war and she came quite irrationally to the conclusion that I had been sent to find out who'd been responsible for the capture of the British airman. If she'd thought about it, she'd have realised that it was unlikely after all these years. She wanted, too, to find out what we knew about the betrayal. In fact, at that stage we knew nothing. But, in coming to see us, she gave us the answer. She came out of guilt and fear because it was she who'd betrayed them, in order to punish the doctor and the girl.

I don't think she saw further than that. She didn't even envisage their deaths or the deaths of the others."

Blanchard sighed.

"I feel pity for her," he said.

"So do I," replied Rudd. "I was sitting here picturing her that day all those years ago, driven out of the house by jealousy that ate into every part of her; perhaps hesitating, as she did this morning, and then crossing the road and going into the German headquarters."

He had seen her quite vividly in his mind's eye; a younger woman, more upright, with those dark eyes under their heavy lids smouldering with a passion beyond her control. How soon had she regretted what she had done? Probably, Rudd guessed, the moment she spoke the words that betrayed them.

Blanchard was saying, "As I was taking her home, she mentioned the roses."

"What roses?" Rudd asked sharply.

Blanchard spread out his hands.

"I didn't quite understand all the story. She was still very distressed and I had to piece it together. But it seems, after the war, she received a letter from England, containing quite a lot of money and a typewritten note, asking her to place white roses on the girl's grave on the anniversary of her death. It seems she's buried in Demour, in the cemetery of the little church of Notre Dame on the outskirts of the town."

"Simone's grave?" asked Rudd.

"I suppose so. She simply said 'la jeune fille'—the young girl." He smiled sadly. "It seems ironic, doesn't it, that she who caused the girl's death should be asked to remember her in this way. She said she goes every year to the grave. She hasn't missed once. But she was worried that perhaps she'd done wrong and this was one of the reasons you'd come from England, making inquiries."

"Was the letter signed?" asked Rudd.

"No," replied Blanchard. "She said she had no idea who sent the money."

Rudd jumped to his feet, sending the wicker-work chair crashing backwards into the boxes of shrubs.

"Phone!" he cried wildly. "I've got to phone England!"

Blanchard looked startled.

"Now?" he asked.

"Yes!" Rudd shouted. "Straight away! My God, I've been blind not to see it before."

"There's a telephone in the café," Blanchard said, getting to his feet.

"Then get me this number," Rudd ordered, scribbling down Bravington's number on the edge of a beer mat. "Do it now," he added, as Blanchard appeared to hesitate, "and reverse the charges."

The telephone was on the wall beside the bar. It seemed to take a long time to get through to the international exchange and Rudd tore savagely at his nails as Blanchard, aware now of the urgency, argued fiercely in French with what seemed to be a whole succession of cantankerous telephone operators.

The waiter, the barman and four old men playing cards at a corner table listened with undisguised interest. They, too, had caught the sense of drama.

Blanchard replaced the telephone receiver.

"They'll ring back when they've placed the call," he said.

"How long?" asked Rudd.

"Twenty minutes," Blanchard replied.

It was the longest twenty minutes that Rudd had ever spent. He drank two brandies and walked up and down the length of the café, his hands in his pockets and his shoulders hunched.

What a fool he had been! The evidence had all been there in front of him. It had only needed a little imagination on his part to realise that love could be a stronger motive for revenge than hate.

And yet, to be fair to himself, how could he have known until Blanchard mentioned the roses.

Roses! My God!

The telephone rang at last and Rudd pounced on it.

"Hello! Hello!" he shouted.

A woman speaking in French said something incomprehensible and then he heard Bravington's voice. It was a bad line. Bravington sounded as if he was at the bottom of the sea.

"Where's Mercer?" Rudd shouted. He listened and caught only the first few words of Bravington's reply. The rest was drowned in a roaring sound like surf.

"What did you say?" bellowed Rudd.

". . . in London," was all he could catch of Bravington's reply.

"But you said something else," Rudd cried. He banged the receiver with the flat of his hand, hoping to clear the line. There was a momentary lull in the background noises, enabling Rudd to hear quite clearly for a short time.

"I said he's in London at the moment but I gather he's returning to Suffolk on the 4:10 train," Bravington repeated.

Rudd glanced at his watch. It was nearly 11:45. He would never make it in time.

The crackling sound returned. With a feeling of desperation, Rudd bawled out his message.

"If you can't stop him from going back, then put a guard on John Thurleigh."

There was a faint interrogative noise from Bravington.

"John Thurleigh!" Rudd shouted. "He lives in the village. Keep him away from Mercer at all costs."

The roaring sound surged up again and, although Rudd banged the receiver several times more, it persisted and finally he hung up in disgust. All he could do now was hope that Bravington had heard him and would take action.

He turned back to Blanchard who was waiting equally tense at his side.

"Get me the airfield," he said. "I want to talk to the pilot who brought me over."

This time the call was put through at once although there was another delay while the pilot was found. At last, he came on the line.

Rudd was brisk and business-like.

"I'm returning to England at once," he said. "See that the plane's ready for take-off as soon as I arrive." As he started towards the door, the man behind the bar, evidently the café owner, began expostulating loudly with Blanchard.

"He says we haven't paid for the drinks," Blanchard explained.

Rudd threw some money down on the counter.

"Is that enough?" he asked.

"More than enough," Blanchard replied.

"Then let's go," said Rudd.

It was a nightmare journey back. Blanchard drove as fast as he could and the hedges, fields and little farmhouses went speeding past in a blur of green and brown.

In Demour, they stopped long enough to pick up their luggage at the Metropole and to say a hurried good-bye to M. Martin before they were on their way again, dodging through the traffic in the town centre and picking up speed again as they reached the outskirts.

Rudd fretted at every delay, at every red light and traffic hold-up and only relaxed when they were out in the country again.

He had scarcely spoken to Blanchard since they left St. Sauveur des Bois and Blanchard, his attention fixed on the road, seemed indisposed to talk either.

It was only when they reached the airfield and were walking towards the plane, which with its engine running was waiting for them, that Rudd broke the silence.

"Thank you for all you've done," he said. "I'm most grateful."

"The case is solved?" Blanchard asked.

"I think so," Rudd replied.

He was certain in his own mind, although there were still many details that needed filling in.

"So the trip wasn't wasted?" Blanchard said.

"No," replied Rudd. "It's been very much worthwhile."

Blanchard smiled, the two men shook hands and then Rudd walked towards the plane.

As he climbed in, he glanced back. Blanchard was standing a little distance away and Rudd could tell by his stance that he was a disappointed man. Evidently he had hoped that Rudd would offer him some explanation. Under the circumstances that would be impossible. Some secrets, not unlike Mlle. Giraud's, could never be told.

A few minutes later the plane was taxiing down the runway and then Rudd felt the slight lift as it became airborne.

Below, Blanchard's trim, well-dressed figure grew smaller and smaller until finally it disappeared from view.

# 14

Bravington was waiting for him as he touched down. He looked a very worried man.

"I hope you know what you're doing," he said to Rudd as the Inspector approached, carrying his shabby canvas holdall. "Who is this John Thurleigh, anyway?"

"I'll explain," said Rudd.

He was hungry and tired. There had been no time to stop for lunch on the way and he felt the past two days had been spent almost entirely in motion. He longed for a meal and an hour's rest. But there was no chance that he would get either.

"We'll take your car," Bravington was saying. "Then we can talk. I've told my chauffeur to follow behind."

They walked to Rudd's car and the Inspector unlocked it and climbed wearily in behind the wheel.

"I suppose you realise," Bravington was saying coldly, "that this John Thurleigh, whoever he is, might have good grounds to bring a case for police harassment?"

"You've put a guard on him?" Rudd asked.

"I did what you told me," Bravington snapped. His usual urbane manner had quite gone; he was coldly and terrifyingly displeased. "I arranged for a police sergeant to call at his house and keep him there. I can imagine we'll arrive to find a very angry man. What possible connection can he have with Mercer? I've never heard you even mention his name before."

"None," said Rudd.

"None!" repeated Bravington.

"That's the whole tragic irony of it," replied Rudd. "There is no connection. I'll explain."

"I think you'd better," Bravington said grimly.

Rudd was silent for a long moment, trying to marshal his thoughts.

"I think," he said at last, "that I'd better begin by telling you what I found out in France. Mercer, as we know, was working at the hotel Metropole during the war and had no connection with the Resistance group in the area apart from the one courier, known as 'S,' who took messages and information from him and passed them on to the wireless operator."

"Yes, yes," Bravington said impatiently. "We know all this."

"In the same winter that Mercer was in Demour, a British plane on reconnaissance flight was shot down over the town and the pilot baled out. He was captured and taken to German headquarters for questioning."

"By Mercer?" asked Bravington.

"No," said Rudd. "I don't think they ever met."

"Then . . ." began Bravington.

"Let me finish," replied Rudd. "It'll make sense in the end, I promise you."

"I sincerely hope it does," Bravington replied. He folded his arms across his chest in a gesture that indicated he would listen but he would not be easily persuaded by what he heard.

Rudd plodded on. He felt like a schoolboy confronting an unsympathetic headmaster who had irrefutable evidence of a misdeed.

Added to this was his own weariness and the need to concentrate on driving the car. Suddenly he doubted his own judgement. Supposing he was wrong, after all? Supposing, like Mlle. Giraud, he was acting out of emotion and stress?

It was too late to withdraw now. The situation had been set up. The police sergeant was with John Thurleigh at that very minute. That, at least, would have to be explained.

"The airman escaped," Rudd continued.

"How?" barked Bravington. He seemed in a mood to doubt even the facts.

"Does it matter?" Rudd asked.

"I think it does," Bravington replied coldly. "You must have evidence to back up your story."

"It's not my story," Rudd said. He felt suddenly angry. After all, he had done his best. He resented being treated in this way. "I got it from two separate sources and I've no reason to doubt its authenticity.''

"Very well," said Bravington. "Let's hear it."

"He escaped," Rudd repeated, "by putting on a German officer's greatcoat and climbing out of the window of the office where he was being interrogated when the officer was called away to deal with some disturbance. He then made his way to a café where he was hidden for a time but, because he was injured, he was moved to a doctor's house in a small town nearby and later to a farm where he was found when the Germans came to search the place. Presumably he was sent to a prisoner-of-war camp.''

He stopped there and tried once more to think the story out. It had made sense, sitting at the café table with Mlle. Giraud beside him in her black hat and dress, weeping, the heavy silver crucifix swinging against her thin chest as she bowed her head.

Would Bravington in his present mood understand what had happened? Would he be able to imagine the emotions and passions that had swept her, and the others, all those years ago, when the grey Nazi uniforms paraded in the streets and no man knew whom he could trust?

Love. Jealousy. Hatred. Betrayal. Revenge. And remorse, too. And pity. And all the suffering. The girl, Simone, who leapt from the third-storey window. The farmer who shot his wife, his children and then himself. The old priest who at last could say quietly, "I understand.''

"The Resistance group was betrayed," Rudd went on, "by the woman who kept house for the doctor. She loved him and she thought he was having an affair with a young girl who brought the British airman, and others, to the house to be hidden.''

Said like that it sounded bald and unconvincing.

"She was jealous," Bravington remarked, dismissing it as all perfectly natural.

"Yes," Rudd replied quietly. "She was jealous.''

"I still don't see where Mercer fits into all this," Bravington went on. "Or John Thurleigh, for that matter.''

They were approaching the village and Rudd gave up all attempts at trying to explain.

"You'll understand," he said, "in good time.''

The houses surrounding the green looked very calm and peaceful in the late afternoon sunshine. It seemed as if nothing could disturb their tranquillity and yet it was here, among the great elms and the cottage gardens, that the last act of the drama would be played out.

"You realise, of course," Bravington was saying, "that I shall have to put in a report about this. I can only repeat that I hope to God you know what you're doing."

Rudd lifted his shoulders resignedly. It was too late to worry about that now. They were in front of Thurleigh's house and there was nothing he could do but park behind the police car that was already standing at the gate and walk up the path to the front door.

It was opened by a police sergeant in uniform, a heavily built man who, like Bravington, looked worried and ill at ease.

"Mr. Thurleigh's at home?" asked Rudd.

"Yes, sir. He's in the sitting-room. I don't know what all this is about . . ."

"You're not supposed to," Rudd replied shortly.

"But he keeps asking questions," the sergeant began, addressing Bravington as Rudd had pushed past him and was walking up the hall. He sounded aggrieved.

"Mr. Rudd will explain everything," Bravington told him. There was a cold and sarcastic note in his voice.

John Thurleigh was sitting at the side of the fireplace reading when Rudd entered. As soon as the door opened, he jumped awkwardly to his feet, throwing the book down on the chair behind him.

"Now, look here," he said. "I demand an explanation."

He was, as Bravington had gloomily predicted, a very angry man. His usual timid and self-effacing attitude had quite gone. Two angry red patches had appeared on his cheek-bones. Then he caught sight of Rudd.

"Oh, it's you," he said, clearly relieved. "Thank God you've come. Perhaps you can explain to that bone-headed imbecile over there in the blue uniform, whom I found waiting for me on the doorstep when I came home this afternoon and who insists on standing guard over me like some lunatic nanny, that I'm a perfectly harmless schoolmaster and, what's more, a citizen of this country with certain irrefutable rights."

The sergeant coloured up at Thurleigh's remarks and shifted his feet about. Rudd, who was taken aback himself by the vehemence of Thurleigh's words, motioned silently with his head and the policeman left the room, stiff-shouldered and with every muscle in the back of his neck expressing personal outrage.

Thurleigh turned to Bravington.

"And who is this man?" he demanded.

Bravington stepped forward and introduced himself. His calm and urbane manner had returned and in the face of it Thurleigh immediately lost confidence. He ran a hand through his thinning hair so that it lay in untidy wisps over his forehead. He was no longer the individual standing up for his rights but an anxious and bewildered man.

"Do sit down. Both of you," he said, waving a hand nervously. "I suppose I ought to offer you tea but, really, I feel so distressed by the whole experience. I do wish somebody would explain exactly what's going on."

"I think Mr. Rudd had better do that," Bravington said, sitting down and crossing his legs.

John Thurleigh looked at the Inspector.

"You? But it makes it all the more bewildering. What have you to do with all this? I thought you were here on holiday."

"So I am," Rudd said, "in a manner of speaking."

He too sat down.

"I'm sorry, John. I don't want to explain anything just yet but I think you'll understand in time. First of all, I'd like to ask you a few questions. You were in the R.A.F. during the war I believe?"

"Yes, I was."

"And you were shot down over Demour, in France, and captured?"

"Ah!" said Bravington, as if he was beginning to see some sense in it all. "So Mr. Thurleigh is your British airman?"

"But all this was years ago," Thurleigh protested. "What on earth has it to do with a police sergeant entering my house?"

Rudd plodded on.

"As I've already said, I don't want to go into details yet," he continued. "Let me summarise the story quickly. You escaped; you were hidden first in a café in the town, then in a doctor's house and later on a farm where you were found and recaptured. Is that correct?"

Thurleigh merely nodded in reply. He looked suddenly tired and sad.

"Would you mind telling me about that incident?"

"Must I?" Thurleigh asked. "It's so long ago and I'd prefer to forget it."

"I think you must," Rudd persisted gently.

"Very well then," the schoolmaster replied. He sighed deeply. "I was taken to a farm. It wasn't much of a place; more of a peasant's small holding. They were a nice couple. They had two little girls, I remember. I was there for about three weeks, hidden in a loft over the barn. The idea was that as soon as my leg was really strong, I'd be moved on again, further south, nearer to the Spanish border. I'm afraid, though, it took a long time to get better.''

He patted the game leg that was stretched out stiffly in front of him. ''In fact,'' he added with a small wry smile, ''it never properly healed.''

''And then?'' Rudd prompted him.

''Then the Germans came. We had plenty of warning of their arrival. The farm was at the end of a long straight road, I heard them coming from a long way off and then I saw them: four motor cyclists, a lorry and a small staff car. There was a gap in the boards of the barn that gave me a good view of the yard below. They drove into the yard and the officer in charge and some of the soldiers went into the house. They were in there for about ten minutes. When they came out, they started searching the out-buildings. Then the officer stood in the middle of the yard and shouted in English, 'We know you're hiding somewhere. Give yourself up or your friends will pay for it.' They'd been good to me, that French farmer and his family. So I came out with my hands up. It was while they were marching me towards the car that I saw the bodies being brought out of the house; the man, Jules, and his wife and the two little girls. They were six and eight years old. The soldiers slung them into the back of the lorry as if they'd been sacks of potatoes.''

He covered his face with his thin hands.

''For God's sake, must we go on with this? Don't you imagine that I still have their deaths on my conscience?''

''Because . . .?'' Rudd began.

Thurleigh looked up and a flash of anger came back into his eyes. ''Because if I hadn't been there, they would still be alive. If they hadn't tried to hide me, the Germans wouldn't have shot them.''

''The Germans didn't kill them,'' Rudd said quietly. ''It was the farmer who shot his family and then himself.''

Thurleigh stared at him.

''Are you sure?''

''That's what I've been told,'' Rudd replied. ''I had it on good authority.''

''I thought I heard shots as the Germans came into the yard,'' Thurleigh said slowly, ''but I couldn't be sure because of the noise of the engines. And afterwards, when they went into the house, one of the cyclists kept revving his bike. I thought that had drowned the sound of the firing. You see, the officer went in with his revolver drawn and the soldiers with him had rifles. I just assumed . . . Not that it makes any difference. They're dead and I must take the blame for it.''

''They knew the risks,'' Rudd replied. He felt he ought to say something to relieve the man's burden of guilt but Thurleigh was not to be comforted.

''No difference,'' he said simply.

Rudd cleared his throat and returned to the subject.

''You were taken away for questioning?'' he asked.

''Yes.''

''And did they ask you about the others?''

''The others?''

''The doctor; the girl who took you to the farm?''

''Of course they asked. But I told them nothing because I knew nothing. I knew no names. They were careful never to tell me their names. I called the doctor 'Monsieur' and the girl 'Mademoiselle.' ''

Again he gave that small tight smile.

''It was all very formal. I didn't even know where they took me, because it was dark when I arrived and dark when I left. The attic where I was hidden in the doctor's house had only a skylight. I saw clouds, nothing else. I certainly couldn't have identified the place.''

His face looked suddenly pained and anxious.

''I suppose they're dead too?''

''The girl is, and the doctor,'' Rudd replied.

''And the café owner and his wife in Demour?''

''They're still alive,'' Rudd assured him.

''Thank God, at least, for that,'' Thurleigh whispered.

Bravington, who had been showing signs of increasing impatience during this conversation, now broke in.

''Look here, Rudd, this is all very well but I don't see where it's leading to. You've established that Mr. Thurleigh was the British airman and, as far as I can see, that's about all.''

''I have only two other questions to ask,'' Rudd said soothingly.

He turned back to the schoolmaster.

''Have you ever met Alec Mercer before?''

''Before he came with you to my house, you mean?'' Thurleigh asked. He seemed quite bewildered by the question. ''No, I hadn't. Look, what has Alec Mercer got to do with all this? I hardly know the man. As a matter of fact, I've not even been inside his house, although he had asked me round to his place for a game of chess tonight."

"I see," said Rudd. His face was totally blank.

"And the other question?" Bravington demanded.

"I beg your pardon?" Rudd asked.

"You said you had two questions to ask of Mr. Thurleigh," Bravington said coldly. "So far you have asked only one. What was the other?"

"Oh yes," replied Rudd. "It's quite a simple one, John. When you were thinking of selling your house last year, was it advertised on the market?"

"I fail to see . . ." Bravington began, but Rudd overrode him.

"If you don't mind, sir," he said, "I'd like Mr. Thurleigh to answer the question."

"Why, yes," the schoolmaster replied, making a small helpless gesture with one hand. "I really don't see the point but, yes, it was advertised. Two or three estate agents had it on their books and then I changed my mind and withdrew it from the market."

"Thank you, John," Rudd said. He got to his feet. "That's all for now."

The two red patches returned to Thurleigh's cheeks.

"This is not good enough," he said firmly. "I cannot allow you to leave without some explanation. As far as I can see, all you've done is ask questions, the point of which I don't understand."

He was trembling as he spoke but he was not without a certain dignity. Rudd looked at him sadly.

"John, I wish I could explain. But it's not my place to do so at the moment. There are other people involved. But I promise you this, that whatever happens, I'll see some satisfactory story is put about the village to explain away the police sergeant. I'll see you won't suffer as a result of it."

"And I must be satisfied with that?" Thurleigh cried indignantly.

"I'm afraid so," Rudd replied.

He walked to the door, Bravington following behind him.

In the hall, Rudd dismissed the sergeant who was standing stiffly at the front door.

"You can go," Rudd told him.

"Now, sir?" he asked.

"Yes, now," repeated the Inspector.

"Very good, sir," the sergeant replied.

He opened the door for them and walked out behind them, jamming his helmet on his head in a manner that indicated he felt he had been ill-used and he deeply resented it. Getting into his car, he drove off in an angry spurt of gravel.

Rudd got into his own car.

"John Thurleigh may have to be satisfied with that interview," Bravington said, getting in beside him and slamming the door shut, "but I'm not."

Rudd nearly lost his temper. I'm tired, he wanted to shout. I'm hungry! I've probably just lost the friendship of a man I liked and trusted. I like this place, too, but the chances are I'll never be able to come here again. What more do you want? My blood?

Instead he said quietly as he pressed the starter button,

"We're going to see Alec Mercer. You'll hear the full story then."

"Now, look here, Rudd," Bravington began, "the whole point of putting you on this case was so that Mercer wouldn't suspect I was involved . . . ."

"There is no case," Rudd said.

"No case? What on earth do you mean?"

"Just that," the Inspector replied. He turned the car into the lane that led to Mercer's house.

"People make the wrong assumptions," he went on, "like Thurleigh, thinking the Germans shot that farmer and his family. And they make assumptions because they don't examine the facts properly. Thurleigh was convinced he was right because that was the way he expected Germans to behave. They shot people. So all these years he's nursed a grudge against them. Perhaps, in some subconscious way, that's what he needed to believe."

"I don't understand," Bravington said. He seemed more subdued now. Something in the Inspector's quiet voice and assured manner had calmed his anger.

"I do," said Rudd. "He needed to believe there was someone else more guilty of their deaths than himself. He still blames himself, as you saw this afternoon, but he had comforted himself all these years with the thought that his wasn't the ultimate guilt. That lay with the Germans who shot them. Don't you see? We're like children in the dark; we need some small candle to comfort us."

"And Mercer? Where does he fit in?" Bravington asked.

"Oh, Mercer," said Rudd. "He needs that light, too. Because, you see, his guilt is one of betrayal."

"You mean Mercer betrayed them?" Bravington protested. "I can't believe that."

"There are many kinds of betrayal," Rudd replied. "I've learned a lot about it in the last couple of days. There's the deliberate handing over of a person to his enemies. And there's the betrayal that's mentioned in the general confession. How does it go? It's such a long time since I've been to church. Something about leaving things not done. I can't remember the exact words."

Dorothy would know them, he thought. Of the two of them she alone had kept alive the strong Anglican faith that had been so large a part of their childhood.

" 'We have left undone those things which we ought to have done, and we have done those things which we ought not to have done; and there is no health in us.' "

Bravington quoted the words quietly and Rudd looked at him in surprise.

"Yes, that's what I meant. It's about the sins of omission."

"And what was Mercer's sin of omission?" Bravington asked him.

"Something quite simple, that the others did, one at least of his own choice: the farmer who shot himself. And the other one who tried: the young girl called Simone who jumped from a third-storey wondow. And all the others that the Germans rounded up: Pierre, and Jules and Little Louis. Unlike them, he omitted to die."

"And because of that he feels that he betrayed them?" Bravington asked.

They were turning into the drive that led to Mercer's house.

"Yes," said Rudd. "Deep down, I think he does. But like Thurleigh, he needs his candle for the dark."

# 15

Mercer's Rover was parked outside the house, so he must have returned from London and collected the car from the garage on the way back. Rudd drew in behind it and, leaving Bravington still in the car retrieving his brief-case from the back seat, the Inspector got quickly out and ran up the steps.

The front door was set open and a big oblong of sunlight fell across the parquet flooring of the hall. As Rudd approached, Mercer was just crossing the hall, dressed in casual clothes. He had had time, then, to change since his return.

Rudd's shadow intercepted the sunlight and before he had time to speak, Mercer turned, saw him and came towards him with every sign of pleasure at the encounter. There was about him that larger-than-life quality that Rudd had noticed when he first introduced him to John Thurleigh; an expansiveness of personality that tended to intimidate other people and make them feel somewhat less than life, as it was probably intended that it should.

"Mr. Rudd! What a pleasant surprise," he began.

A second later he caught sight of Bravington getting out of the car and coming forward towards them.

In that second, Mercer's whole demeanour changed. It was as if a light had been switched off, leaving him utterly blank. His expression was like that on the face of a dead man, composed only of features, wiped clean of any human vitality.

The next moment his personality was switched on again, but now it was changed. The warm expansiveness had gone. The deliberate smile of welcome was replaced with a wry quirk of the mouth and above it his eyes were very hard and watchful as he greeted Bravington.

"I had no idea, Felix, that you two knew each other," he said.

Bravington did not reply but made a dismissive gesture with his hand, as if disassociating himself from Rudd's company. Mercer's smile grew wider. It seemed to the Inspector that there was a small bright centre now in his eyes, concentrated and cruel; or it might have been simply a trick of the light.

So that's how it's going to be, Rudd thought. A duel between the two of us with Bravington standing on the side-lines. He felt his tiredness fall away. If that was the way it went, then he would see that he made the most of the situation. It was with an almost jaunty air that he said,

"Yes, Colonel Bravington and I are quite well acquainted. You don't mind if we come in, do you?"

"Of course not," Mercer replied, still smiling. "I was about to have tea in the garden; very English and civilised. Do join me."

They followed him into the study and through the open French windows that led on to the terrace. As they passed, Rudd noticed that the broken lock had been replaced with a new one.

Tea was already laid. As Mercer had said, it was all very English and civilised. Garden chairs were grouped round a table that had a large sun umbrella over it. There were scarlet geraniums in the ornamental urns that topped the terrace steps, and the lawn, neatly shaved now, sloped gently down towards them.

"Sit down," Mercer said. He seemed amused by their presence. Bravington, on the other hand, had retired behind the stiff mask of a face that Englishmen assume when they are feeling ill at ease and on the defensive. He would not even glance in Rudd's direction but totally ignored him.

Rudd did not care. Let Bravington act the offended parent if he wanted to. The Inspector had no intention of being stood meekly in a corner as punishment.

"A scone?" Mercer was asking, passing plates. Bravington accepted one in silence. Rudd drew his chair nearer the table and took a huge bite from his.

"Very good," he said appreciatively.

"Mrs. Blair makes them," Mercer replied.

The little piece of polite conversation fooled neither of them. Rudd grinned and Mercer suddenly laughed out loud. Bravington looked away up the lawn, his profile very magisterial and disapproving.

"I've been in Demour the last couple of days," Rudd said in the same conversational tone of voice.

"Really?" said Mercer. He was pouring tea from a big-bellied silver teapot and the steady stream of liquid from the spout did not waver for a second.

"I stayed at the hotel Metropole," Rudd went on, "at M. Martin's invitation. The son, of course, of the proprietor who was in charge when you were there during the war."

"Felix, you've been talking out of turn," Mercer said to Bravington, his voice gently chiding.

Bravington looked angry.

"I had no intention that you should find out anything about this; Inspector Rudd had definite instructions. However, since he's taken it upon himself to divulge what he knew to be in strictest confidence, I can only say, Alec, that I did what I thought best to protect you."

His glance fell momentarily on Rudd, cold and implacable, and then, with terrible deliberation, he looked away.

"I'm afraid Colonel Bravington isn't too pleased with you, *Inspector* Rudd," Mercer remarked, putting an ironic emphasis on the word "Inspector."

"And I'm not too pleased with him. I made it quite clear that I needed no protection. I'm more than capable of looking after myself. However, let's keep the party polite. I hate recriminations. I'm quite prepared to overlook the whole matter."

"It's not as easy as that," Rudd said in his best official manner. "Not when it's a question of a man's life being in danger."

"Mine, you mean?" Mercer said, laughing. He had recovered his poise and his air of well-being. "Surely you don't mean all that nonsense about the photograph? Felix, I'm surprised at you. I told you when you asked me about it that it was the work of some crank. Do you mean to say you took it seriously and put poor Inspector Rudd on guard duty?"

It was Rudd who answered him.

"I took it seriously, Mr. Mercer. I jumped quite naturally to the conclusion that someone on that train of prisoners, or someone connected with one of them, intended killing you for the part you'd played in that war-time incident. You'd received other photographs and threats, Colonel Bravington told me. It seemed one attempt was made on your life. Then you moved here. Your car was shot at. Your house was broken into. Someone, too, I discovered had made a hide-out in one of the old fishing huts by the river. But to me, it

added up to a revenge more personal then an anonymous face among
a crowd of prisoners. The photograph was therefore a bluff. But a
bluff intended for whom? For you, presumably. The person who
sent the photographs and the threatening letters wanted to fool you
into thinking that the incident on the railway station was the motive
for the revenge. But that didn't add up. You, better than anyone
else, would know who was likely to want to kill you. Only you
knew whom you had betrayed. We couldn't ask you, of course.
Colonel Bravington had made it quite clear, as he said, that you
weren't to know you were being watched. So I had to assume that
you might in fact be aware of the real identity of the man who
threatened you but, for your own reasons, you wished to deal with
him yourself. But I couldn't take that risk. My job was to see you
didn't get killed and that was why I went to Demour, to try to pin an
identity on this unknown person who hated you enough to wait thirty
years before finally finishing you off and even then, when he had
run you to ground here in Barnston, was prepared to play with you;
to make three attacks that weren't meant to be serious in order, as I
thought, to break your nerve.

"The obvious answer seemed to lie with the Resistance group
in Demour. They had been betrayed. Perhaps, I told myself, one of
its members thought that you were responsible. You had, after all,
been playing the part of a German sympathiser as part of your cover.
What about the person called 'S' who acted as your courier? Could
he have suspected that you were a double agent? I asked a lot of
questions of various people, M. Martin among them, and I found out
a good deal of information that at the time seemed irrelevant. I
heard, for example, a fascinating story about a British airman who'd
been shot down over Demour and hidden by the Resistance group.
Unfortunately, it didn't seem to fit in with your activities. The man
was recaptured, sent to a prisoner-of-war camp and that seemed to
be the end of it. As far as I could see then, he had no connection
with you at all. You hadn't even met him. You know him now,
though. The man was John Thurleigh.''

Mercer put down his cup on the table and made a gesture with
one hand to indicate incredulity.

"Really?'' he said. "How extraordinary!''

"No,'' replied Rudd. "Not extraordinary at all. You intended
meeting him. In fact, you used me to introduce you to him. It was
all part of the cover story.''

"What cover story?'' Mercer asked. He was suddenly angry.
His face was blanched with fury and the nose and chin jutted out,

taut and bony, under the covering flesh. He turned to Bravington. "I don't know what the hell this bloody Inspector of yours is drivelling on about, but I refuse to sit here listening to this bloody stupid farce any longer! I will not tolerate it! I will not!"

He had risen abruptly to his feet and the chair in which he had been sitting, and which in his anger he had thrust violently behind him, fell backwards with a crash on to the paving stones.

Bravington looked up at him. He seemed quite unmoved by this show of temperament.

"You'll sit down again, Alec," he said quietly. "Mr. Rudd seems to think he has a theory and, before I leave, I intend that he shall substantiate it with some evidence. Go on," he added, turning to Rudd, "I want you to present your case."

Strangely enough, Rudd found his austere reasonableness more intimidating than Mercer's loss of temper. Here was a man who could not be bluffed or persuaded. He was the type of top-ranking Civil Servant who had got where he was on pure intellectual ability that, keen and sharp as a surgeon's knife, would cut through a lesser man's pretence. He wanted facts. He wanted it all in black and white and Rudd did not have that kind of evidence.

"As I told you in the car," he said, "there is no case."

Mercer, who had refused to sit down again, had walked across to the far side of the terrace and stood leaning against the low wall that divided it from the lawn. With his arms folded across his chest and his face partly in shadow, accentuating the hollows of his cheeks and hooding the deep-set eyes, he looked like some gaunt Indian war-chief, forbidding, cruel and utterly contemptuous.

"No case?" repeated Bravington, raising his eyebrows. "You can hardly expect to get away with that, Mr. Rudd. When I called you in on this affair, we already had some evidence to justify an inquiry; the incident in the garage, the photograph and the threatening note sent to Mr. Mercer. You saw the last two yourself. You can hardly deny their existence and tell me there is no case."

"I'm not trying to," Rudd replied. "All I'm saying is they weren't part of a threat against Mercer's life. It was all a bluff from the beginning. A car may have reversed in actual fact, causing him minor injuries, or he may have faked the whole thing. I'm not sure about that. But I'm sure of one thing: it wasn't an attempt on his life."

"And the shot fired at his car?" Bravington insisted.

"A bluff, too."

"Oh, come on!" Mercer cried, bursting out laughing. "It was

kids, I tell you, with an air-gun. No-one's going to take a potshot at a car with an air-gun and hope to kill the driver.''

"Exactly," said Rudd. "That was the whole point."

Bravington shook his head slightly as if humorously bemused by Rudd's reply.

"I'm afraid I don't quite understand you," he said with devastating courtesy.

"I didn't understand it myself until this morning," Rudd admitted. He had the sensation of wading through deep water. Every step he took now in telling the story was going to be an effort. In the face of Mercer's contempt and Bravington's cool civility, he felt like an outsider, a non-member of a club, trying to win approval; which was ridiculous. After all, he knew he was right. Nothing else, otherwise, made sense.

"Mercer received a photograph and a threatening letter," he repeated. "He made light of it at the time but he made sure that there was someone in the office when he opened it. You heard about it, Colonel Bravington, as you were intended to do. He told a story about a car reversing into him. You questioned Mercer about it. He refused to take it seriously. In fact, he got angry when you suggested he should be protected. But he knew very well you'd put some sort of watch on him. You couldn't do otherwise. Security demanded it.''

"Are you suggesting that he knew he was being watched?" Bravington asked incredulously.

"Of course," Rudd replied. "You rumbled me, didn't you, Mr. Mercer, the day you moved into the village and you joined me at lunchtime outside the Plough? You knew I'd been planted so you decided to make use of me. I thought it a bit strange at the time that you suggested I might introduce you to one or two people in the village. But my own vanity stopped me from seeing the obvious. I thought my own cover story was so damned good that you wouldn't see through it. Oh, I know you put up a convincing display when the Colonel and I turned up here together this afternoon. But you weren't surprised. You were shaken, yes, because you realised something was up. You sent the photograph and the letter to yourself, didn't you, because you wanted to be watched?''

"Oh God!" cried Mercer, throwing up his hands. "Are you going to take this rubbish seriously, Felix? The man's off his head."

"But there were other copies sent . . ." Bravington began, ignoring Mercer and concentrating on Rudd.

"He *said* there were others," Rudd replied. "You only have his word for it."

"But the other evidence?"

"If you mean the shot taken at his car and the attempted break-in," the Inspector said, "they were rigged. He fired at the car himself, while it was stationary. I should have realised that myself as soon as I saw the damage to the door panel. The dent made by the pellet was too round, too perfect. If the car had been moving when it was hit, there would have been signs of a glancing impact. You can work it out mathematically if you like, allowing for the speed of the car and the velocity of the pellet but, as the panel's been repaired, you'll have to take my word for it."

"And how do you suggest I faked the attempted break-in?" Mercer asked in an insolent tone. "You were with me in the room when we heard the crash in the study next door as the lamp was knocked over. Or are you suggesting, perhaps, I had an accomplice? Mrs. Blair, for instance?"

"M. Martin at the hotel Metropole gave me the clue to that," Rudd replied. He had settled down now and was even beginning to enjoy the situation. Mercer's contempt meant nothing to him now. "He found you one day during the war, fixing up a hidden microphone in the chandelier in a private dining room used by the German officers. You were threading a wire, he said, down through the ceiling from your bedroom on the floor above. If you remember, Mr. Mercer, on that evening of the so-called break-in, you were standing at the cabinet pouring drinks at the moment of the actual crash as the lamp fell. The cabinet backs on to the party wall between the two rooms and the lamp was standing on a bookcase directly behind the cabinet. I think you performed the same trick; a piece of wire threaded between the two rooms. It only took a quick tug on one end, the end concealed in the cabinet, and the lamp was pulled to the ground. The main light in the study wasn't working; conveniently, of course. You used a torch to see by and I had only a glimpse of the room; the lamp lying shattered on the floor and the French window open with the lock broken. You didn't intend I should see any more at that stage; not until you'd had time to clear away the wire and mop up the pool of water on the floor in front of the open window. I noticed it at the time but didn't attach much significance to it. Thinking it over later, it did strike me as strange that it should be such a large pool of water. I know it was raining hard that evening. That, again, was convenient for you and you made use of it. If you remember, you invited me round for a drink that same morning, after the weather forecast had predicted a change in the weather, because the rain suited your purpose very well. If I'd insisted on calling the police, as indeed I did and as indeed you counted on my doing, then a downpour of rain would have made tracker dogs useless, as you yourself pointed out. What would you have done Mr. Mercer, if it hadn't rained? Used a lawn sprinkler, left it on all evening, so that the grass was wet enough to confuse any scent? Because, of course, you couldn't run the risk of the dogs leading the police handler straight to you. That would have been very awkward, wouldn't it?

"But to get back to the pool of water. As I said, it was a strangely large puddle considering the break-in had only just occurred. We know now, of course, that it hadn't. You'd forced the lock yourself earlier in the evening before I arrived, and the rain had been driving in for a couple of hours. You hoped I wouldn't notice. You daren't run the risk of faking the break-in too early and besides, you wanted me at ease, with a few whiskies inside me, before the crash came. I was to be a witness but a witness in a darkened room, mellow with drink, rushing out after you into the garden, chasing some non-existent burglar, confused by it all; but not confused enough to be unable to back up your story when the police arrived. But you were damned careful to have the pool of water wiped up and the remains of the lamp cleared away, with any tell-tale fragments of wire, before they came."

"Do you intend listening to any more of this nonsense?" Mercer broke in furiously, addressing Bravington. "Because I for one don't know what the hell he's talking about with his pools of water and his bloody hidden wires. And what was I supposed to be witness to, for God's sake? Why the hell should I go to all that bloody trouble to fake a break-in?"

"Because you intended to use my statement later as evidence," Rudd replied. "Evidence to cover up a death."

"Whose death?" Bravington asked sharply.

"Ask him," Rudd replied, nodding at Mercer. "Ask him why he put the air-bed and the blankets in the old fishing hut. They were meant to be found, of course, as further evidence that there had been a real threat to your life, Mercer; that someone was, after all, intending to kill you and therefore you had good reason to carry a gun. But here you were in a bit of a dilemma, weren't you? If you made those early attacks look too serious, the place would have been swarming with police. They'd've put an official guard on you, not someone like me just ambling about the place; and you couldn't do what you intended to do with a bobby in uniform standing on your doorstep. So the attacks had to look questionable at the time; something you could shrug off when they happened. Only afterwards, when you were ready, they could be used as proof that you had good reason to believe your life was in danger, after all. And I was to be used as backup man to this cover story which, I might add, I believed in myself until this morning.

"You see," he went on, looking directly at Mercer, "you were so convincing that I took it all seriously. I really thought your life was in danger and that it was my duty to find your potential killer. So I went to France and there I found out about the betrayal of the Resistance group and the British airman, John Thurleigh. You knew of the same facts yourself but you didn't examine them quite carefully enough because, out of your own feelings of guilt because so many of the others had died, you wanted, indeed you needed, someone you could blame. Let's look at the facts now. John Thurleigh was hiding on a farm at Ternes. The Germans pounced there first, rounded him up and took him in for questioning. The doctor at St. Sauveur des Bois was arrested next, where the airman had been in hiding before he was moved to the farm. Then others were captured; Pierre, the schoolmaster's son and Little Louis. From them, the chain of arrests led back to Demour, to 'S' who had been your courier and then to Boileau, the wireless operator, and Marcel Gavin, the group's leader, and to the others. And that chain of betrayal began, you believed, at the farmhouse at Ternes. It couldn't be the farmer. He'd shot himself and his family as the Germans arrived. So it had to be the airman, John Thurleigh, who betrayed them.

"But you were wrong, you know. He knew nothing. He didn't even know their names. You should have looked elsewhere for your traitor. John Thurleigh was innocent. I found out what you in thirty years didn't, Mercer: the real identity of the person who gave them away. But I want to make it quite clear that you will never get me to turn traitor myself and betray the secret. That person is old now and broken under thirty years of guilt. If you had looked into that face, as I have done, you would have been amply revenged."

"I wanted revenge?" Mercer asked. He pushed himself erect away from the wall and came to stand over the Inspector. "It's a ridiculous theory. Interesting and ingenious but ridiculous just the same. You accused me of not looking at the facts. Aren't you falling into the same trap yourself? What did these people mean to me? As you know very well, I had no direct contact with them. I simply passed on messages. I agree, it's a terrible thing to think they were betrayed and died as a consequence but these names you mentioned, Pierre, Little Louis, I didn't even know of their existence. Why should I want, therefore, to avenge their deaths?''

"Not *their* deaths," Rudd said. Mercer towered over him, standing between him and the sunlight so that Rudd could not see the expression on his face. "Only one death, Mr. Mercer. You accused me just now of not looking at the facts and I will admit that I made one basic wrong assumption from the start. I assumed that your contact with the group, the courier known as 'S,' was a man. It was a natural mistake to make but a foolish one. I might otherwise have arrived at the truth a little earlier. Because 'S' wasn't a man; it was a girl, a beautiful, dark-haired girl called Simone who jumped from the window of her flat as the Germans arrived to arrest her and who died later under interrogation and whom you loved, as only a solitary man like you can love, deeply and for ever. So for thirty years you planned to avenge her death just as you planned to keep her memory alive with white roses on her grave.''

"Oh, God!" said Mercer and blundered back against the table. Rudd and Bravington both jumped to their feet at the same moment, the Inspector picking up the fallen chair that still lay on the terrace, Bravington guiding Mercer into it.

"I'll get some brandy," Bravington said briskly and disappeared through the French windows into the house.

Mercer wept. Rudd sat silent beside him, remembering the other occasion that day when Mlle. Giraud had cried in that same broken and helpless manner.

Bravington returned with a glass of brandy which he thrust into Mercer's hand.

"Here, drink this, man," he told him.

They heard the rim of the glass rattle against his teeth as he lifted it to his mouth.

"They tied her to a chair," he whispered. "Did you know that? She was terribly injured internally but they tied her to a chair to keep her upright while they questioned her. She took a week to die. Another prisoner told me. He'd been in the cell next to her.''

"And you thought John Thurleigh had betrayed her?" Rudd said quietly. Mercer looked up at him, his face twisted with grief.

"What else could I believe? That her friends gave her away?''

"So John Thurleigh was to die," Rudd said. "When did you plan it to happen, Mercer? Tonight, when he came here to play chess?''

"Yes," Mercer said in a low voice.

"Shot in the garden?" Rudd persisted. "Mistaken for an intruder?"

"Yes."

"And I was to supply the back-up evidence," Rudd added, addressing Bravington. "Mercer kept a watch on Thurleigh for years, found out where he lived, planned that one day he'd meet him face to face and kill him. He must have had his name down on the local estate agents' lists, waiting for a house in the area to come up for sale. Then came the first set-back. A house did come on the market, but it was Thurleigh's. Mercer must have been furious at that. He'd run the man to earth and now he was proposing to move somewhere else. Then Thurleigh changed his mind about selling. The house was withdrawn from the market. Mercer decided to wait a little longer. Then, it seemed, his luck changed. This house came up for sale. He was all set to act out the revenge that he'd been planning for thirty years and hadn't been able to follow through because he was abroad."

He turned back to Mercer.

"What would you have done if you couldn't buy a house in the village? Shot him anyway? Faked another break-in, only this time in Thurleigh's own house? Or, perhaps, used the car routine, only this time with a high-velocity rifle aimed to kill? After all, whatever you did, there was little chance you'd be implicated. Thirty years is a long time. The police would never have dug back that far, looking for a motive."

Mercer would not answer but averted his face. After a moment of silence, Bravington touched Rudd on the arm and drew him to the far side of the terrace.

"What do we do now?" he asked the Inspector. He seemed totally at a loss.

"Nothing," replied Rudd. "As I told you, there's no case. Thurleigh is still alive. We know Mercer intended killing him, but where's the evidence? I have only a theory. Besides, I think he's suffered enough."

Bravington glanced back at the figure of Mercer slumped in the chair under the gay umbrella.

"We leave it there, then?"

"I think so," Rudd replied.

"There are ends to be tied off," Bravington pointed out. "Thurleigh will want some explanation for a start."

"I'll square it," Rudd said.

He thought suddenly of the schoolmaster. What would he say to him? Some lie, of course. But their relationship would never be quite the same again.

"And Mercer?"

"I'll persuade him to come back to London," Bravington said. "I'll find him something to do, some special assignment; take his mind off things, you know."

"He won't forget," Rudd replied. "After thirty years of remembering, it becomes a habit."

As with Father Tabard and Mlle. Giraud, the past could never be forgotten.

Although perhaps, Rudd thought, as he walked quietly away round the side of the house, Mercer might one day be able to say, as the old priest had done, "I understand."

## ABOUT THE AUTHOR

JUNE THOMSON'S previous Detective Rudd novels include *The Habit of Loving*, *Death Cap*, *Case Closed* and *A Question of Identity*. She lives in the beautiful Essex countryside outside of London.

# WHODUNIT?

Bantam did! By bringing you these masterful tales of murder, suspense and mystery!